Muzzled

June Whyte

A Kat McKinley Greyhound Mystery
Book 2

White City
Press

Books by June Whyte

Sex on Tuesdays

THE GUMSHOE CHICK MYSTERY SERIES
Gone to the Dogs
For the Love of Dogs
Doggone It!

VETS 2U MYSTERY SERIES
Murder at Kangaroo Downs
Death at Dingo Creek
Homicide at Emu Lodge

KAT MCKINLEY GREYHOUND MYSTERIES
Chasing Can Be Murder
Muzzled
Hounded
Leashed

CHIANA RYAN CHILDREN'S MYSTERIES
The Case of the Disappearing Corpse
The Case of the Missing Dinosaur Egg

www.amazon.com/author/junewhytebooks

Muzzled

June Whyte

This edition published by White City Press
An imprint of Misti Media LLC
https://www.mistimedia.com
Available in both Paperback and eBook Editions
1 2 3 4 5 6 7 8 9 10
Text Copyright © June Whyte 2024
Cover Copyright © 2024 by White City Press
Paperback ISBN: 9781963479416
eBook ISBN: 9781963479263

1

I WAS IN A TEN-PLUS LIP LOCK WITH Ben Taylor, the guy I'd want to be having sex with if ever the world came to an end, when the phone rang.

Ben's steamy lips lifted half an inch from mine. "Do we have to worry about that?"

This question didn't rate an answer. Instead I forced his wayward lips back into their favorite position—velcroed to mine. Then, just as Ben's tongue and fingers became so-creative and oh-so-hot I was on the verge of a scream, the high-pitched shrill of the phone let loose again.

Frustrated, Ben broke contact. Arms slumped to his sides, he rolled his eyes toward the ceiling, and, ignoring my small whine of disapproval, took a step backwards. "Go on," he growled giving me a small push in the direction of the irritating sound. "Answer the damn thing. Whoever it is obviously isn't going away."

I swung across the room toward the kitchen table where the handset of my cordless phone vibrated and trilled like a love sick dove. Damn. Damn. Damn. Why hadn't I performed mass murder and drowned all my IT appliances in the goldfish bowl when Ben dropped by to see if I could *lend him a bowl of sugar?*

Before snatching the phone from the table, I turned to fire a mock scowl at Ben. "Do. Not. Move," I told him and waved an admonishing finger in his direction. "Give me two seconds. I'll inform whoever this is that I don't need any of whatever they're trying to flog and I'll be right back. Okay?"

Ben's grin of acquiescence was pure unadulterated Wicked. Sent shivers to places where shivers shouldn't go. He draped himself in a languid, *I'm-waiting-wench-so-get-your-ass-into-gear* pose against the closed door of the pantry then folded his arms across his snug fitting black T-shirt. A T-shirt that declared him King of the Rats. His muscles bulged, stretching the material across his chest like a second skin. Not fake gym muscles like you see on ads for taking vitamin pills or selling Stairmasters and treadmills. These were *Real Man* muscles. Muscles acquired outside in the rain, wind, and sun, training greyhounds, helping his brother Nick with the cows, chopping wood, or any of the multitude of jobs associated with running a working farm.

Up until a couple of weeks ago, Ben and I were nothing more than *mates*. You know—the sort of mate who makes up a foursome at cards on a Friday night when one of the regulars can't make it. The sort of mate who fills you in about the newest treatment for bone fractures advised by some expert on the online greyhound forum. The sort of mate who steps in and helps catch a killer when your life is threatened.

A damn good mate.

Yep. That's how it was before Ben noticed I had *womanly* attributes. Like boobs. Admittedly not poke-your-eyes-out boobs—more the pancake variety that improve when I remember to wear my Wonder Bras—but definitely female boobs. And that under my workday attire of jeans and baggy sweatshirt lurked a woman who had designs on taking *mate-ship* several levels higher.

Consequently, while snatching the phone's handset up from the table, in my mind I was already ripping Ben's body-hugging T-shirt over his head and exploring the highs and lows of the six pack and other delights lurking beneath.

Almost salivating, I placed the phone to my ear, eyes still feasting on the man most likely to end up in my bed—or on my kitchen table, within the next ten minutes. "Kat McKinley," I snapped, eager to murder the cold caller before he/she got started on their rant.

"Hi, you don't know me." The young male voice on the other end of the line sounded hesitant. "I'm calling about your sister, Elizabeth."

"Liz?" I hadn't heard from my sister in almost a year. Her way of saying *I love you and I'm thinking of you* was to send a Christmas card fashioned from something resembling toilet paper each year. Last I knew she was living in one of those modern-day communes somewhere in Queensland. *Somewhere* being the operative word. "Okay, what trouble is Liz in this time?"

"She's disappeared."

"Like in *poof* or she just up and moved on without telling you?" I sighed. Like she normally did.

"Um… I'm not sure."

This was getting us nowhere and Ben had shifted from the cupboard and was now bending over, head in the fridge, the denim of his jeans cuddling his gorgeous rear end. I gritted my teeth. "Okay, where exactly did my sister disappear from? And who the heck am I talking to?"

"Sorry. I'm Liz's friend, Scott Brady. We were paired off at the Rainbow Commune up near Townsville for just over a year and when she got bored and moved on, I thought, why not, and moved on with her. We hitched rides with truckers for awhile and then, about three months ago, stopped wandering and settled down."

"And where exactly did you settle?" Ben, eyes burning hot coals as he watched me, was now licking a strawberry flavored ice-cream off a stick.

"Port Augusta," said Scott. "I'm helping out at the greyhound track here and Liz is squatting in an empty rabbiter's shack, about ten miles out of town—"

"You're joking!" I broke in, dragging my eyes from Ben's assets as anger kindled and burned in my chest. "My sister has been living in Pt. Augusta, in South Australia, in the same state as me, for the last three months and she hasn't bothered to contact me?"

There was a shrug in his voice. "You know Liz."

"I certainly do." Anger at how little my sister cared about me made my voice harder than I intended. "And believe me Scott, there's nothing to worry about. What's happened is my kid sister just woke up one morning, thought the grass was greener somewhere else, and left you. I'm sorry. Nothing personal. She does it to everyone."

"But—"

"Don't worry about Liz. She's a survivor. Manages to do so by caring for no-one but herself. If you want my advice, for free, go find yourself another girlfriend. Forget Liz. She's evidently forgotten you." By now, Ben had removed his top and was slowly rubbing strawberry ice-cream across the smooth contours of his chest.

Oh. My. God.

"Sorry, Scott. Gotta go." My fingers loosened their grip around the hard plastic and the phone slid to the floor.

Within seconds my T-shirt had joined Ben's on the kitchen lino and my body was plastered like wallpaper against his hard toned torso.

Oh yeah…and strawberry ice cream had never tasted so good.

2

An hour later, like a kid on a soda high, I danced along the dusty track leading to the temporary dog shed that housed my team of racing greyhounds. The birds were singing. The bees were buzzing. And it felt great to be alive. After sixty sizzling minutes spent exploring mind-blowing *Kama Sutra* positions with Ben, I couldn't wipe the smile from my lips.

I did a shuffle-ball-change beside the abandoned ride-on-mower pushed to the side of the pathway, and twirled like a ballerina. And why would I want to lose my smile? I'd fancied Ben as more than a good mate for over a year. Now he was my lover and I couldn't get enough of him. Like a leading lady from one of those soppy musicals on the Movie Channel, you know, *Singing in the Rain* or *West Side Story* or *Oklahoma*—I burst out singing.

"Oh what a beautiful morning…"

An ugly feral cat, peering furtively up at me from the middle of an overgrown geranium bush, hissed her disapproval. This was the cat that constantly hung around the property, her sole ambition in life to tease my dogs, get them riled up and barking. She gave me a narrow-eyed sneer, flicked her half-a-tail in the air and scuttled off in the direction of the wood pile.

Evidently didn't appreciate my unique singing voice.

Undeterred by the cat's display of negativity, my thoughts returned to Ben. Big Ben. Agile Ben. Naked Ben. After claiming his *bowl of sugar*—in fact make that *three bowls of sugar*—Ben had gone home. Reluctantly. Said he had to prepare his team for the afternoon's racing at Gawler.

I ran a nervous hand through my already messed up hair. The thought of today's race meeting, in which I had four dogs nominated, immediately brought my euphoria down several notches. After an enforced spell, it was imperative my dogs started winning races again. If not, I'd be getting a visit from my crusty faced bank manager—not for a cup of tea and a chat—but to confiscate the keys to my house. In his will, my father had left me enough money to put a healthy deposit on my property, but there was still the bank loan to pay off.

Due to a psychotic ex-owner, Peter Manning, who not only tried to murder me but also set fire to my beautiful brick kennel house, burning it to the ground, my greyhounds had been temporarily out of work and consequently, at the moment, money was in short supply.

The memory of that all-consuming fire followed by an attempt on my life, still peppered my dreams at night. Peter locked me inside a coffin at his father's funeral home, his plan to press the button that sent me and the coffin on a one-way journey to the crematorium. Not only was I lucky enough to survive Peter's dastardly plans, but after he'd been charged and incarcerated, my friends pitched in and knocked up a temporary dog shed to house my racing team until the insurance company got around to building a new kennel house in the blackened rubble.

Mind elsewhere, I glanced up in time to see Jake, my young dreadlocked kennel-helper, wave as he wheeled his five-speed racer through the front gate. I waved back. After closing the gate behind him, Jake propped his bicycle against a pepper tree and went to check on Stella, one of the two rescue greyhounds I currently cared for from the Greyhound Adoption Program. There were two kennels near the front gate, built to house GAP dogs waiting to be re-homed as pets. Jake was probably checking to see if the greyhound bitch was comfortable after yesterday's spaying operation.

I'd collected Stella from the vet's surgery the night before and would drop her brother Stanley, the other GAP dog off as soon as he came back from being 'cat tested' at his current foster home. All greyhounds in the program are neutered and socialized before being placed in their new homes. That way the dogs settle down and aren't tempted by the smell of a local bitch in heat, or in Stella's case, be a problem because she *is* the local bitch in heat.

Leaving Jake to assess the condition of Stella's ten stitches, I continued on down the path toward the dog shed. The thought of those stitches instigated a sudden image of my sister, Liz, age four, a row of ugly black stitches marching across her forehead. The little minx had trailed me up a tree in our back yard, slipped, fell and cut her head. I was at the ripe old age of eleven at the time, an age where I needed to escape my kid sister's constant chatter. But no—Liz had to follow me up that tree. All I could remember now was how brave she'd been while the doctor stitched her up. And her sweet smile when Dad and I brought her home from the hospital and I promised to read her a story and stay with her until she drifted off to sleep. I sighed. When we were kids I couldn't move without stumbling over my baby sister. And now—she couldn't even ring to let me know we were living in the same State.

As usual, my greyhounds were excited to see me. Excited? Make that ecstatic. Hyper. Over the moon. After calming them down, I set to work. First I collected the four sets of registration papers needed for the day's meeting and placed them on the table. If I forgot their papers my dogs wouldn't be racing.

Intent on grooming my runners before leaving for the track, I lifted a blue cotton bag featuring a picture of Snoopy from a hook on the back wall. Brushes, combs, rags and grooming mitts spilled out onto the table as I upended the bag onto the table. It was a matter of pride that made me particular about the appearance of my dogs. In fact my greyhounds usually looked better than I did when we went racing.

After opening the lid on a bottle of baby oil, I reached into the cupboard for my set of nail clippers. Should I be worried that Liz had moved on without telling Scott? Should I ring Ma to let her know? My globe-trotting mother and her latest beau, Dwayne, were holidaying somewhere in Europe. *Somewhere* being the operative word. I sighed and snaffled a collar and lead from a nail on the wall. If I rung Ma now and told her I was worried about Liz's disappearance, it would be like banging my head on a steel rubbish bin. She'd merely spout the same old line: *Elizabeth Jane can look after herself. She closed the door on this family five years ago when she took off without a word and didn't come back.* Always conveniently forgetting it was Ma's constant nagging and belittling that sent Liz off into the world at sixteen, two weeks after our father Jake McKinley was run down and killed by a road train. For some reason Ma had been jealous of Dad's closeness to us girls—more so Liz—and tore strips off her at every opportunity. Without Dad around to blunt the verbal blows, I guess my little sister saw no reason to hang around. Liz had drifted from commune to commune over the last five years with only a card at Christmas to let us know she was still alive.

And now, it seemed like she'd drifted someplace else. Again. This time leaving a boyfriend behind. Typical Liz. Frustrated, I pushed my nomadic sister from my mind and unfastened the nearest kennel door. "Okay, your turn to be prettied up, Lofty," I told the big brindle greyhound, the most talented greyhound in my racing team. Lofty, or Big Mistake, if you wanted to call him by his racing name, previously belonged to Peter Manning, the guy who'd tried to kill me, but since Peter had been incarcerated, Lofty, plus Peter's other dogs had been sold. Now, big ugly Lofty was owned by my mother. Yes. Amazing—but true. Of course I had all sorts of trouble locating Ma when Peter Manning's dogs were put up for sale but I figured no way could I lose the best dog in my kennel. Naturally, it took charm, guilt and even a little blackmail to cajole Ma into buying the dog—especially as she ranked the job of greyhound training alongside scrubbing toilets, drug dealing and prostitution, but in the end she'd agreed on one condition. If Big Mistake didn't win her outlay back in the next twelve months, I'd quit training greyhounds and get a 'real job'. Her words not mine–and something she'd been pushing for ever since Dad died.

A rough wet tongue greeted me when I stooped to fasten a collar around Lofty's bull neck. "Hey, cut it out," I told him and wiped the drool from my cheek with the back of my hand. "I've already washed my face today, big boy, so you can haul that flannel back in your mouth. Okay?"

Heeding every chiropractor's sage advice, I wrapped my arms around the dog's body and bent my knees ready to heft the dog's forty five kilos up onto the treatment table. Of course, Lofty, not known for his eagerness to assist in difficult situations, decided to turn into a bag of concrete blocks.

"Want a hand there, dude?" Jake, his grin a mile wide, barreled through the doorway.

"'Ts okay. I'll manage," I puffed, wrestling Lofty's dead weight onto the table before stepping back to rub the trembling muscles in my arms. "Are Stella's stitches okay?"

"Stitches looking good, dude, but she's down in the dumps. I think our little GAP dog's missing her bro."

"No worries. I'll collect Stanley from his foster home tomorrow. That'll make her happy again."

As soon as Lofty was settled on the table, I lifted each paw and carefully snipped the tiny points off the dew-claws on the insides of his wrists. Didn't want to risk the claws breaking off or tearing the skin if he sustained a bump on the track. Satisfied with the results, I wiped his coat over with a rag dampened down with baby oil, rubbed him dry with a soft towel and then used a soft brush to smooth his brindle coat down flat.

While I groomed, Jake wrestled a broom from the equipment at the back of the shed and swept the cement floor—all the while giving a badly off-key version of some rapper-dude. One of six professional protesters who bunked down in contented squalor in a rented apartment half hour's bike ride away, Jake adored my greyhounds as much as they adored him. As usual he was dressed in ancient torn-at-the-knees jeans and one of his many *Save the...* T-shirts. Today's faded and out of shape model proclaimed his anxiety for the endangered tree frog. Jake's tuneless warble didn't seem to worry the dogs. In fact, every canine in the kennel house had settled, head on paws, eyes soft, to listen.

That is, until a piercing squeal of brakes broke the serenity of the shed. Immediately, the dogs hurtled off their beds. The shed exploded in a cacophony of barking. And Lofty leaped off the table and bolted.

"No Lofty!" I grabbed for the loop at the end of his lead and hung on as he dragged me through the open doorway.

Fair dinkum, if a forty five kilo dog sets his mind on heading in a certain direction, puny girl muscles fall well short as a deterrent. Like a programmed missile, Lofty rocketed along the path toward the front gate. The leather lead bit into the soft flesh of my fisted hand. And my upper body struggled to keep up with my running feet.

"Slow down, Lofty!"

I may as well have yelled at the sky.

"Some geriatric dude's stealing Stella!" Jake gasped, incredulous, as he caught and passed me in a blur.

Almost tripping over a rocky garden border when Lofty decided to take a short cut, I squinted up ahead at the two kennels at the end of the path. "But he can't do that—"

Evidently he could. One of the kennel gates was wide open and an old guy, dressed in tight purple pants and a monster of a Hawaiian shirt, so bright it could be classed as a lethal weapon if you weren't wearing sunglasses, was running out the front gate with the GAP dog spilling from his arms.

A cold chill skittered up my spine and my heart gave several quick lurches of fear. If he dropped Stella, her stitches could burst.

"Hey, you! You can't just come in and take one of our adoption dogs. You have to fill out an application."

Lofty barked in agreement and gave a hard yank on the end of his lead. It was like he was saying: *Just let go of me, dude, and I'll rip those purple pants right off that guy's backside!* I told Lofty I couldn't take the risk because he might break a toenail while performing a service to the community and I needed him fit and sound for today's Country Cup heats at Gawler.

Dismissing my worries, he put his head down and pulled harder. I dug in my heels, spewing gravel up behind me like a surfer riding a wave. If I didn't stop for oxygen—right this moment—my chest would split down the middle like a dropped watermelon in a game of catch. In desperation, I reached out with one hand, latched onto a tree branch and held onto the branch while Lofty choked and bucked and skidded to a head-shaking halt. His frown of frustration said it all. Especially when I wrapped the lead around the trunk of the tree, tied it in a knot and left him to bark his disapproval while I hurled myself in the direction of the fashion disaster dog-napper.

Reaching the gateway, I stood there, bent double, breathing hard, unable to believe the scene in front of me. A nondescript, pus-colored Holden car of vague vintage wheezed and roared on the other side of my front gate. Its exhaust proclaimed it was in dire need of replacement and the tar scent of hot engine filled my nostrils. My dude-helper, Jake, who had reached the gateway before me, sat on the ground holding a handkerchief to his bleeding nose while the old guy in the car slammed his foot on the gas and skidded off in a cloud of smoke.

"You okay, Jake?"

"Yeah, dude," he said, slowly getting to his feet, handkerchief still attached to his bleeding nose. "Sorry I couldn't stop the wrinkly from nabbing Stella. Thought I could take the old dude out, easy like, but the bastard used a knuckle duster."

I peered into Jake's eyes to see if he appeared concussed but all I could make out was a high level of indignation. Probably from being taken out by a geriatric, forty years his senior. "Not your fault," I reassured him. "But you'd better go raid the ice-tray in the dog fridge.

Then sit down, lean your head back and put the ice pack on the back of your neck."

When Jake shuffled off, my thoughts returned to the audacity of the dog-napper. This guy, who had the fashion sense of a constipated rocker, had a lot to answer for. Stella, the GAP bitch he'd kidnapped would be horrified by the man's rough handling, especially as the poor dog was recovering from her spaying operation and consequently nursing ten stitches. Like a pressure-cooker simmering on high, anger bit deep into my gut. With no gun to shoot out the dog-napper's tires, all I could do was shout obscenities as I watched the piece of shit car disappear into the distance.

"I'll get you, you no-good, bandy-legged creep! And when I do, you'll be eating soup through a straw." *Even if I had to put out an SOS email to Scuzz, my seven-foot biker bodyguard buddy, and tell him to jump on his hog and get his leather clad ass back here. His services were needed.*

Frustrated, I untied Lofty and turned toward the kennel-house. No good going after the thief—by the time I found my car keys he'd be long gone. Instead, I'd ring the police and report Stella's kidnapping. Get them to look out for the pus colored Holden. Put out an all-systems alert. Notify their SWAT team if necessary.

After returning a disgruntled Lofty to the safety of his kennel, I settled the dogs with a slice of cheese apiece and hurried into the house. What was the old guy in the Hawaiian shirt up to? And why steal Stella? The brindle bitch wasn't a racing proposition any more. Worth no more financially than a slap up meal at the local pub. I frowned as I snapped open the front door and charged inside. Something wasn't right. Stealing a pet GAP dog was too weird…unless the jerk thought Stella was one of my racing dogs.

That troubling thought sent a sudden icy coldness seeping into my bloodstream. It was as though I'd never feel warm again. To be honest, the whole situation freaked me out. Plus if I didn't leave for the racetrack soon, kenneling would be finished, my dogs would be scratched, and I'd be up for a hefty fine and a bollocking from the chief steward.

And zero chance of adding to my bank balance.

Head in a whirl, I collapsed on the comfortable overstuffed sofa set in the middle of the lounge room. My racing dogs were my life, my job, my love. Sensing my distress, Tater, my tiny stegosaurus-hearted Chihuahua and Lucky, my wriggly black greyhound pet decided they both wanted to sit on my lap to comfort me. Tater snuggled on with ease but Lucky, after two unsuccessful attempts, leaned her head on my knees and looked up at me from under her eyes with a troubled frown.

"Don't worry, I'll sort this out," I told my canine friends before pulling out my cell phone. Finger on the first 0 of the standard 000 emergency number, I hesitated. Perhaps I should ring Detective Inspector Adams, personally. He'd been the policeman in charge of the case when Peter Manning, my psychotic ex-owner dragged me into his crazy murderous schemes. I'd feel more comfortable talking to a policeman I knew.

But would he remember me? Would he get all upset and snarky if I called him on his private mobile number? I screwed up my nose. Gently teased one of Tater's tiny ears between the tips of my fingers. Perhaps I should ring my best friend, Tanya, first. Or contact Ben—get his input? Then, mind zeroing in on the terrified expression on Stella's face and the nasty smile on the thief's, I started punching in DI Adam's number.

3

A car screamed to a halt outside, horn blaring loud enough to waken fossilized dinosaurs. I shot from the sofa—phone tumbling from my fingers. Holy catfish! If that was a police car—Detective Inspector Adams must have the telepathic powers of the part-faerie barmaid, Sookie Stackhouse. A snarling Tater immediately went into his usual guard dog pose, hair vibrating all along his back, growl deep in his throat, while big soft Lucky scuttled behind the sofa, long ratty tail between her legs, paws over her eyes.

Could it be Purple Pants returning to steal another one of my dogs? Heart skipping several beats, I stashed my cell in the back pocket of my jeans and sprinted to the front door.

One step through the doorway I stopped. Paralyzed with dread. I tried to yell, but the sound stuck in my throat. All I could do was stare in silent horror as a stony-faced Purple Pants hauled Stella from the car, and as though she was a piece of garbage, tossed the dog over my front fence.

"No—" My throat closed over and a red hot fire invaded my chest as I raced across the yard to the whimpering Stella—in time to see Purple Pants thrust one arm through the open window and gesture with an arrogant middle finger. In time to hear tires gouge the bitumen as the pus-colored Holden slewed from one side to the other and took off up the road. In time to inhale a nose full of exhaust fumes.

Before I could close my gaping mouth, a fire-engine red Toyota Yaris, a car reminiscent of a matchbox toy, spun in through the gateway and came to a four square halt beside me. Out of the car, like an avenging angel, tumbled my best friend, Tanya Ashford and her eleven-year-old daughter, Erin.

"What's going on? Did the dog get run over? Who's the *wrinkly* who took off in the crap car?" Tanya's rapid fire questions could barely be heard over the roar of the disappearing Holden.

"It's Stella." I squatted to check on the miserable brindle greyhound bitch lying in a heap at my feet. "And that *wrinkly who took off in the crap car* stole her and, deciding she was faulty, brought her back." I gazed up at Tanya and shook my head in disbelief, struggling to stem the tears prickling like hot daggers behind my eyes. "He-he just tossed her over the fence, Tan!"

"Come again?"

"That piece of shit threw Stella over the fence." The red hot fire burning in my chest turned white. "If I find him I'll kill him—tear off both his arms and beat him over the head with the bloody appendages until he stops breathing—and then I'll kill him."

"Hallelujah!" Tanya stood, hands jammed hard on hips, eyes flashing. Her body language screamed retribution. With that one word—hallelujah—I knew, without a quibble, Tanya would hold the geriatric thief down while I kicked him repeatedly in the nuts.

Turning away, I cupped Stella's face in both hands and planted a kiss on her long nose. In return, two sorrowful brown eyes met mine and a rough tongue licked its way across my cheek.

"Did you get the car's rego, Kat?" Tanya hunkered down beside me, her fingers reaching to smooth Stella's brindle fur.

"The plate was dirty." I closed my eyes trying to visualize the car's number plate. "I think the first two numbers were seven and three and there was what looked like a V somewhere in the mix."

"Might be enough to find an address. Anyway, I'll ring my mate, Paul Simmons—ask him to check it out on the police data base."

"Paul Simmons?" I frowned. The name rang a distant bell.

"Yeah. Remember that star footballer I dated back in high school?"

Still frowning, I shook my head.

"Well, I ran into him a couple of weeks ago and guess what—he's a cop now—*and* he owes me one."

A hazy image of a fresh faced high-school footballer's woebegone expression after Tanya dumped him flashed into my mind. "Dated? Tan, you gave the poor guy his marching orders two days into the relationship."

All nonchalant, Tanya shrugged one shoulder and stood up. "Anyway, as I said, we caught up again recently and got to talking over a cup of coffee at *Rivers*, you know that new restaurant on Philip Highway, and Paul admits the dumping was his fault. He knew the most important rule I dated under—*never ever stand me up*."

I shook my head at her. Tanya might be my best friend in the world and a powerhouse to have on side in times of trouble, but she still had the ability to leave me open-mouthed, gob-smacked at times. "If I remember rightly, the reason Paul stood you up was because he was called away to the hospital. His mother had been in a car accident and was in intensive care. The poor guy sent you a text from the hospital and rung several times afterwards to apologize."

"Yes, I know Paul was sorry at the time, but aren't you forgetting something?" At my duh look, Tanya continued. "Because Paul stood me up that night I made the mistake of my life." When my duh look intensified Tanya glanced surreptitiously at her daughter who was leaning against the door of the Yaris, completely absorbed in her new Smart Phone and likely discussing how to make petrol bombs with her 2001 *Facebook* friends. "Kat, think about it. That was the night I let Dan tempt me into his bed."

Suddenly the penny dropped. Being in Dan's bed that night instead of at the movies with Paul had changed the course of Tanya's life.

"As I said," Tanya reiterated, "Paul owes me one."

"You're right there." Noticing two of Stella's stitches had burst, I added, "And if Paul comes up with an address for us, I say we pay the dog-napper a visit. See how *he* enjoys being tossed over a fence."

Erin, phone cemented to one hand, strolled across to stare at the blood seeping from Stella's torn stitches. The baby skin between her eyes wrinkled. "How 'bout we toss that bad man in a prickle bush instead?"

"You bet, pumpkin," I said. Although Tanya's daughter and I were always at loggerheads, after Ben and I rescued her from a couple of lowlife thugs who kidnapped her and locked her in a dark cupboard, she and I had come to an amicable understanding. She was still a pain-in-the-butt but she was *our* pain-in-the-butt–and we loved her. "And if there are no prickle bushes around," I promised, "we'll improvise. Okay?"

Erin's evil grin was a carbon copy of her mother's. "Better still, let's like, chuck him into a hive full of angry bees."

Tanya slung one arm around her daughter's shoulder and drew her closer. "Good idea, cupcake. Or what about a piranha infested river?"

"Both options are fine by me," I said giving the nearby gate a vicious kick as I stood up. "At the very least the man will be eating custard through broken teeth."

When Stella let out another soft whimper I bent and scooped her into my arms. "I'm taking Stella inside to clean her up. Got time to help?"

"You betcha."

With Tanya and Erin tagging along behind, I lurched up the path in the direction of my front door, all four of Stella's limbs sticking in the air like table legs.

*****

Naturally Tater and Lucky behaved like it was the social occasion of the year when I brought Stella into the lounge room and lowered her onto the sofa.

"New friend, guys," I told the bouncing twosome. "And she's hurt. So be gentle, okay?"

Lucky immediately raced into the kitchen and came trotting back with her new purple squeaky toy lizard which she presented to Stella. Tater, not to be outdone, strode around the room, head up, tail cocked, a picture of cool. Probably eager to let the newcomer see he was a Hugh Grant lookalike—only shorter.

"Why would anyone want to steal a greyhound they could legitimately adopt?" Tanya mused as she selected a bottle of Betadine from my ever-present first aid kit, broke a bag of cotton balls with her teeth and placed the bottle and the open bag on the coffee table beside me.

I shook my head, every bit as confused as Tanya. "All he had to do was fill out a GAP application form and buy the dog."

"And why bring her back a few minutes later?"

"Got me." I finished bathing Stella's torn stitches and tipped a few drops of Betadine onto a cotton ball. "None of it makes sense."

Tanya chewed on her bottom lip and you could almost hear her brain ticking over as she snagged the basin of bloody disinfectant water and emptied it into the sink. "Unless he stole the wrong dog."

"You mean he thought he was stealing one of my racing dogs?" I blew the bangs out of my eyes. "But which one? The only brindle dog I have racing at the moment is Big Mistake and although Stella's brindle, no-one could mistake her for Lofty. For a start, he's eighteen kilos heavier than her. Plus he has all those extra bits and pieces girl dogs aren't born with."

"Still, it might pay to apply extra security around Lofty—just in case he *is* the brindle greyhound the dog-napper's after."

I gave her a thumbs up. "I'm ahead of you there, Sherlock. There'll be a new super-lock fitted on Lofty's kennel as from today."

After I'd finished attending to Stella, Tanya collected the used cotton balls, dropped them into the pedal bin under the kitchen sink then moved across to the room to give me a quick hug. "Sorry, Kat, but I've gotta get going. Will you be okay?"

"Yeah. No sweat. And thanks for your help."

"I'd hang around in case the dog-napper came back but my shift at *The Luv Bug* starts in half an hour and I gotta drop Erin off at her Dad's first."

"That's okay, I'm racing at Gawler, but hey, we'll find this guy, and when we do, we'll kick his ass to Sydney and back. No-one messes with my dogs and gets away with it."

"Right on, girlfriend." Tanya stooped to rescue her hot-pink faux Gucci handbag from Lucky's mouth before sending a grin in my direction. "Hey, d'ya remember that young stud who often pops into my shop to test the new products—you know, the guy who looks a lot like *Angel* from the *Buffy* series?"

I nodded. How could I *not* remember someone who looked like *Angel*?

"Well, he's trialing our new range of blow up bimbos this afternoon." She wiggled her eyebrows as she ushered her social-network obsessed daughter in the direction of the front door. "Last time he trialed a new product, *The Luv Bug* was overflowing with drooling women and we sold out of the new merchandise in an hour." Tanya winked. "Shame you can't come along and watch."

"Tempting," I said regretfully. "But if I'm not driving out of my gateway and heading toward the Gawler dog track in the next ten minutes I'll have the Chief Steward breathing all over me. And he won't be drooling over my alluring curves and scintillating sex appeal. Oh no. He'll have me reaching deep into my hip pocket to pay a hefty fine— and that's after scratching all my dogs from the meeting."

4

Even though I donned my Superwoman cape and made do with a two minute shower, dragged cotton knickers up over still-damp skin with one hand while drying my hair with the other—and even though Jake loaded the dogs in the trailer for me and secured their registration papers in the glove box of my car—it still took me twelve minutes to get ready. I'd have made it in five if Lucky hadn't taken a fancy to my best pair of mandatory black track shoes. With no time to check more than half a dozen of her 101 secret hiding caches, I finally settled for wearing my second best track shoes, the pair with the split in one toe.

So…when I skidded through the gate and past the pissed off guy with the misshapen cowboy hat who was manning the ticket box and wriggled into the last empty space in the trainer's car park at Princes Park, Gawler—beside a washed-out, grey Ford Falcon van with *Clean me* scrawled across the dirty back windows and a caterpillar-like ten-berth dog trailer attached—it was one minute to kennel-closing.

Yikes!

A curl of dust stalked the tractor as it dragged the sand track in preparation for the first race. Ben, his normally laid back features creased in a frown, came loping toward me. He had the left front door of my trailer open and a collar fastened around the canine occupant's neck before I'd even switched off the engine. "Where've you been?"

"Long story," I told him and grabbed two more leads and muzzles before rocketing from the car. No time for explanations. Not even time to tuck my plain white shirt into the waist band of my requisite black trousers.

Ben urged the first dog to jump down from the trailer then lobbed the lead at a mate who always helped him out at the track. "Here, Bazz. You take Witchy Woman?"

"Her rego papers are in my glove box," I called out and tossed him a blue denim kennel mattress before he took off at a run toward the kennel house.

"Get that one through, mate, and Kat and I'll be right behind you."

With that, Ben snaffled another lead and opened the second door on the left side of the trailer while I managed the two dogs on my side.

Naturally, friendly ribbing from fellow greyhound trainers followed me as I made a mad dash toward the checking-in steward at the door of the kennel house.

"What happened, Kat? Lose your way?"

"Someone musta nodded off to sleep in the bubble bath."

Air tight in my chest, dogs bouncing on the end of their leads, I lengthened my stride and ignored them.

"Hey, Katrina, darling, if Benjamin's wearing you out in bed, you can pass him over to me. I'm always up for it." Of course that remark from Mary Parker, aged in her early forties and dressed like a teenage slut, made me pause long enough to fire a lethal laser glare in her direction. A glare that screamed: '*Leave my man alone…or die!*' With anyone else my glare would have blistered skin—Mary merely ran a seductive tongue over her bottom lip—then smirked.

Once my dogs were checked by the stewards, weighed, vetted and settled inside allotted cages on their own mattresses, I let out a relieved sigh.

"Dunno about you, but I'm ready for a sit down," I told Ben before setting off for the track's covered enclosure which housed numerous

TAB terminals, three bookmakers' stands, the stewards' room, the bar and the track cafeteria.

"Okay, give," said Ben and dragged out a chair from the nearest empty table. He lowered his long frame onto the industrial-gray metal seat. "What kept you?"

"What kept me?" I repeated and let out a sigh as I leant back in my chair, relishing the sensation of a few moments' inactivity. "Well, Benjamin—I guess it's been, what-you'd-call, one of those mornings."

He wiggled his eyebrows suggestively and grinned. "And…?"

I laughed at his not-so-subtle hints of our *athletic* morning activities. "Nah. It's what happened *after* you swaggered off into the sunset that caused the problems."

"Hey, I don't swagger."

"Yes, you do."

A cheeky grin spread across his face crinkling every one of his laugh lines. "No, babe, it's called walking-like-a-man-who's-just-experienced-a-death-defying-ride-on-a-roller-coaster-and-barely-survived."

I let out a chuckle. "You win. No way can I beat *that*." The laughter in Ben's eyes had me itching to get up and go sit on his lap, just to feel his body against mine again.

"So, now we've got *that* established," he went on, eyebrows doing little bitty pushups, "what happened after I left?"

When I filled him in on the Purple Pants saga, Ben's lips thinned. His hand moved to cover mine as he leant across the table. "You okay, babe?"

I nodded, the warmth of his fingers around mine, making me teary. I sniffed and blamed my hormones.

"This creep an acquaintance of yours?"

"God, no!"

"What's he look like?"

I screwed up my nose. "Old guy done up like a neon light and driving an ancient Holden that sounds like a bulldozer. I didn't get the complete rego number but Tanya reckons it's enough for her cop friend, Paul, to find the owner's address on the police data base."

"And once you get hold of this thug's address—no way will you be trotting off to question him on your own—" He paused, chocolate colored eyes boring into mine. "Right?"

I scowled at him. He scowled back. Then, after jerking my hand from his grasp, I raised my eyebrows and peered at him sideways. Was Ben trying to dictate what I could and couldn't do?

"Because *I'll* be with you." At that Ben smiled. A slow, gorgeous, eye crinkling smile that made me wish we were still at home, alone, in my bedroom, with the graphics from page 48 of the *Kama Sutra* open on the laptop beside us.

As a slow steady thump sent heat trekking to the pit of my stomach and juices to parts of the anatomy I won't bother mentioning, I licked my lips and ran my fingers through my hair. Ben's grin widened. He knew what I was thinking.

Oh boy! I glanced at my watch and scrambled to my feet. Time for the handlers involved in the first race of the day to collect their dogs from the kennel house and prepare them for racing. Plus, if I didn't move away from Temptation Incarnate right this moment... I'd do something I'd regret later, like take Ben on top of a table in the middle of the betting ring at the Gawler track with a couple of hundred spectators cheering me on. Hell, the chief steward would throw the book at me. And it wouldn't be the *Kama Sutra* either. More like *Crime and Punishment.*

Before I could move off toward the kennel house to collect Witchy Woman for the first race of the day, an open maiden for dogs that hadn't yet won a race, Bob and Marjorie Sanders, two of my favorite owners, bore down on me.

"Hi Kat. How do you think our boy, Clark, will go today?" Bob asked, goosing my cheek with a noisy kiss. "Worth risking a couple of thousand on him?"

Before I could answer I was engulfed in the comforting scent of vanilla as Bob's wife, Marjorie, clasped me in a bone crunching bear hug. "Don't bother answering that old fossil, dear," she said. "Just ignore him. He's pulling your leg. I swear—some days my eighty five-year-old husband acts like he's going through delayed adolescence." She tutted and rolled her eyes. "Two thousand dollars? We'll be investing our usual two dollars each-way on Clark—regardless of whether he has a chance or not." She stepped back and eyed me with concern. "It's good to see you at the track again, dear. Are you well? Recovered from what that evil man tried to do to you?" She shook her head, tightly permed gray hair like a silver helmet. "If I had my way, he'd be sleeping on a bed of nails every night and never see the outside of a prison again."

"I'm fine now, thanks, Marjorie. And glad to be back racing." I smiled at the two representatives of the RSL Aged Care facility, the syndicate that owned one of my best up-and-coming young dogs. White haired, in their eighties, and devoted to each other, Marjorie and Bob never missed an opportunity to see their dog race. Win or lose, the lively couple treated each outing like a festive event. In fact, when Clark, known to his race-track fans as Wonder Boy, qualified for the final of the Derby a couple of months ago, the RSL organized buses to bring all the residents of the Home to the track. Unfortunately that didn't eventuate. Due to the ferocity of the fire that burnt my kennels to the ground, Clark, like all my greyhounds, had been suffering from smoke inhalation and had to be scratched from the Derby final.

Leaving the Sanders husband and wife team to regale Ben with humorous stories of their exploits at the Retirement Home, I joined the other seven handlers with dogs engaged in the first race. Even after this morning's stressful activities, I couldn't wait for the meeting to start. To me, training and racing greyhounds was up there with Christmas— losing your virginity—winning the lottery—a date with the delectable Hugh Jackman…

Okay, okay, maybe cancel the last one.

But hey, you know what I mean. The thrill of watching those beautiful canine athletes gallop around the track, striving with every sinew and muscle, gave me goose bumps. No matter how many times I watched greyhounds in action—it was always an enormous buzz.

My first entrant for the day, Witchy Woman, a black brindle bitch with snow white paws, wriggled and leaped in the air like a firecracker while I struggled to fit a stretchy pink lycra rug over her head and ease it down across her back. It was like she was saying, 'for Woof's sake, just let me onto the track so I can show 'em how good I am'.

"Okay, Witchy, not long now," I told her and gently tugged her ears. "How about saving all that enthusiasm for the race?" As usual, the wriggling ball of energy ignored my advice. I shook my head at her like a proud Mama with a recalcitrant but gifted child as she bounced outside into the parade ring on the end of her lead. After letting her empty out I trotted her briskly up and down on the grass to warm and stretch her muscles. Box eight should suit the little black brindle bitch as she was a wide runner. Not overly fast out of the traps, she had a powerful finish and I hoped, as she matured, she'd become a handy distance proposition.

After placing my dog in the starting box nearest the outside fence, I stood back with the other handlers and let out a shaky sigh. *It was all up to Witchy now.* The lure approached, the lids lifted and, as predicted, my girl jumped last. *Please don't get hurt.* Mouth dry, I watched as the little dog stayed wide on the track, negotiated the first bend without trouble and once she found her balance in the back straight, began to lengthen stride. *You can do it, Witchy!* Although still a pup and at the beginning of her racing career, this bitch was awesome to watch. In full stride she was a perfect example of the old cliché— *poetry in motion.*

"Go girl!"

And go she did. In the back straight Witchy lay fifth—when she rounded the home turn and passed me at the boxes she was third—by the time she crossed the finish line she was two lengths in front and pulling away.

A massive run—and a welcome addition to my bank account.

After that it was as though my greyhounds had sprouted wings and could do no wrong. From three dogs to race, Witchy and Clark were winners and the unplaced dog, Bugs, who was knocked out of the race on the first turn, still managed to rattle home for third. From my 50% share of the prize money I had enough to pay last month's overdue mortgage, cash to pay the feed man and maybe buy a new tire for my car.

I couldn't stop smiling.

Lofty was in the last race of the day, the best-eight nominated for the Gawler division of the Country Championships. If he won today, he'd represent Gawler against the winners of the other country tracks in the final.

After waiting for Chris, the vet on duty, to apply a one inch track-leg bandage to Lofty's left hind leg, I floated into the parade ring. Couldn't douse my enormous grin. Hey, if this *winner's high* could be bottled, people would queue at their state's Greyhound Racing office to apply for a license. Much healthier than popping pills, sniffing white powder or smoking weed. I smiled at Lofty—a picture of canine arrogance strutting on the end of his lead. A short-priced favorite to win the race, you'd swear the dog had studied the bookmakers' odds and listened to the tote fluctuations on the radio.

It was as I paused by the railing to let Lofty cock his leg and scratch dirt over his back—show those punters leaning over the fence what a fine specimen of greyhound he was—that I spotted a flash of purple toward the rear of the spectators. My heart stopped, my stomach lurched toward my cracked black shoes and my grin melted and trickled off my face. The color purple? A man was talking to Big Mick Harrison, a bookmaker. Just a blur of purple and then he was gone.

Ben sauntered up beside me, bringing his usual practical warmth and reassurance with him. "You okay?" he said, one hand resting on the head of a lightly framed fawn dog in a red racing rug. "You look like you've seen a ghost?"

"I think I have." A shiver skittered through me as I peered at the crowd gathered around the parade ring. "Did you see him?"

"See who?"

"The old guy in the purple pants I was telling you about earlier. You know, the creep who stole Stella." I tightened my hold on the leather lead and edged the dog closer to my side for protection. "Maybe he's after Lofty now."

Ben shook his head, a look of bewilderment on his face. "Why would he be after Lofty?"

"'Cos Lofty's red brindle, just like Stella."

"That's not a reason to steal a dog. Come on, Kat, you're imagining things. A geriatric guy wearing purple pants to a greyhound track would stand out like a neon sign. If he was out there, we'd see him."

"Maybe, but it makes more sense that he'd be after Lofty than a GAP dog." After all, I know what I'd seen and it was definitely a flash of purple. And what about my gut feeling? I'd be foolish not to trust instincts. When I'd gone off alone to meet Peter Manning, I'd ignored my gut telling me things weren't quite kosher—and look where that landed me. Inside a pale blue satin-lined coffin at Peter's father's Funeral Home. No. The new Kat McKinley was more street wise.

Less trusting.

I snorted inwardly as I thought of the way Peter had accused me of being naive and too nice, as though *niceness* was a debilitating disease. Well, if nothing else, this gal learned from her mistakes.

Alert to my surroundings, I vowed to do whatever it took to protect Lofty. Even if it meant paying a locksmith to install a foolproof lock on my temporary kennel house. I loved the big ugly dog. He was the star of my racing team. A great character. And oh yeah, he now belonged to my mother and if anything happened to my mother's dog and she didn't get her outlay back via his race earnings, she'd not only string me to the nearest gum tree by my ears—I'd have to give up training greyhounds.

And that was unthinkable.

The steward at the gate who was calling entrants to line up from one to eight ready to go out onto the track, broke into my musings. Ben gave my shoulder a quick squeeze before positioning his dog beside the gate, first in line, while I tacked on the end with Lofty, who was wearing the pink rug, number eight.

As I followed the rest of the field out onto the track, I took a deep breath and let it out slowly in an attempt to disperse all toxic thoughts. Ben was right. It was probably a woman in purple slacks talking to the two men. Two wins and a third—things were going great today and I shouldn't let a flash of purple in the crowd spoil my euphoria.

But what if Purple Pants was here at the track? What if at the end of the race he grabbed Lofty and threw him in his piece-of-shit car and drove off with him?

Oh, God…the deep-breath-letting-out-toxins trick wasn't working. Okay, time to appeal to the big guns and ask the Universe to take over. Think positive thoughts and allow karma to replace stress. Easier than reciting your A-B-C. Everything was going to be fine. No-one could get to Lofty while we were at the track. Enjoy the success.

Dragging these thoughts along with much needed air into my lungs, I followed the officiating steward and the other seven handlers past the starting boxes and on another fifty meters along the track. Hey, no-one could hijack Lofty while we were surrounded by people. I dredged up a smile. However, as we turned and made our way back along the track in readiness to load the dogs into the metal starting boxes, I couldn't stop myself from scrutinizing the faces of the people lining the fence. You, know—just in case. And the fact that I checked the color of every pair of slacks, jeans, trousers and track-suits on the way, well, that was just plain common sense.

"Good luck everyone," I said after we'd loaded the greyhounds into their respective boxes, closed the doors and stepped up onto the viewing steps.

All around the air crackled with nervous energy as we held our collective breaths waiting for the lids to rise.

A cheeky grin creased Ben's face. "And may the best dog win—even if the best dog *is* mine."

"Pull the other one, Benno!"

"Ya gotta be joking, mate. That bag of bones of yours couldn't run out of sight on a dark night."

Ignoring the good natured ribbing around him, Ben widened his grin into a cocky taunt. "Hey, at least he doesn't need spectacles to *find* the lure like your mutt, Jimmy. My dog, Cool Customer, is a sure thing. Reckon he'll win by the length of the straight."

Ben's nose squished and his dark eyes twinkled. Ooh, be still my heart. He looked so cute. If we weren't surrounded by stewards and trainers I'd have stood on tiptoe and kissed him right on the tip of his squishy nose. Especially as that slutty Mary Parker was draping herself all over him and batting her eyelashes at him.

I sent her a lethal *hands-off-my-man* glare and elbowed Ben in the ribs. "*Your* dog win this race? In your dreams, Benjamin."

Before Ben could retaliate, the mechanical lure, situated on the rail, fired up with a high-pitched buzz that sent the dogs over the edge, barking and scratching at the grill to get out. As the lure roared past the starting boxes, the lids shot open. I held my breath. Would Lofty jump? Or would he miss the start and find trouble? I needn't have worried. The pink rug a fashion statement on his red brindle body, Lofty pinged from the outside box, cut straight across the field, and was two lengths in front before they'd passed the winning post the first time around.

I grinned up at Ben. Now it was only a matter of by how far the big ugly dog would win.

Thirty point eight seconds later, Lofty galloped past the post in full stretch and the race caller declared Big Mistake the winner by six lengths. What a star! What a champ! In two weeks' time, he'd be Gawler's representative in the final of the Country Championships.

However, instead of lifting my euphoria to an all-time high, the win sent my heart fluttering like a trapped moth inside my chest.

What if I couldn't keep Lofty safe until then?

5

Ever increasing traffic snarled bumpter to bumper along the main road winding out of Gawler—a once peaceful country town—now no different to any other over-populated suburb.

The thrum of engines labored in slow gear with the honk of impatient horns as I turned off into a back street where hundred-year-old houses rubbed shoulders with modern square blocks of cold concrete. The local fodder store, still showcasing a hitching rail out front, came into view; its grey stone walls roughened by a century of harsh Australian weather. I drove past, inhaled a deep breath, savoring the rural smell of chaff, bran and sweet smelling hay.

"Don't fret," I told Stanley, the red brindle greyhound balancing precariously in the back of my station wagon—between four newly purchased bags of kibble and several tins of powdered milk. As I drove over the outdated railway bridge leading out of the sprawling township of Gawler, a passenger train roared underneath, its destination, Adelaide. I waited until Stanley could hear me again before continuing. "Just a couple of quick snips and it will be all over," I assured him. "You won't feel a thing, and just think—after that you can move in with a lovely family and maybe have a couch to sleep on in the living room. Maybe even some children to play with."

The dog didn't look convinced.

On the way home from the track I'd picked up Stella's brother, Stanley, from his foster home with, a lady who lived in a hundred-year-old cottage in the heart of Gawler. The tall elegant dog had passed all his GAP tests with ease, including tolerating cats, little fluffy dogs and allowing his foster mum to remove his food before he'd finished eating. He'd even been presented with a special green collar to show he could be walked on the streets without a muzzle now.

There was only one procedure left to face before Stanley was ready for his new adoptive home. The one I was attempting to downplay—neutering.

As though seeking more reassurance, and who could blame the poor guy, Stanley stretched his neck forward and licked my left ear with his hot rough tongue.

"Hey, that tickles." I laughed and gently pushed him away, then tightened my grip on the steering wheel to maneuver the car around a large concrete roundabout and onto the new highway. "We'll pay a visit to the vet tomorrow, okay? Not today. Lofty, Witchy, Clark and Bugs are tired and hungry. We need to get them home out of the trailer and into their warm comfortable beds, pronto."

As though understanding every word I said, Stanley's tongue scorched a hot damp trail across the sensitive skin at the back of my neck. I reached behind with one hand and ruffled his ears. "I know, I know, that's fine with you. You're not in any hurry to visit the vet either."

By the time I pulled into the Angle Vale shopping center and parked the car and dog-trailer outside the delicatessen where I always bought ice-cream for the dogs after racing, tiredness enveloped me. I was so looking forward to the familiar sight of my own front gate topped by the sign that said, *McKinley Greyhound Kennels*. It had been one heck of a day. What with Ben *borrowing several very energetic cups of sugar*, the mystery of why and who stole Stella, worrying whether the dog-napper actually had his beady eyes on Lofty, plus the excitement of winning three races—I was all ready for a night in—with the kennel-house double-padlocked, my front door secure and my feet up.

Maybe watching something light and fluffy that didn't overtax my tired brain, like *Death at a Funeral.*

When I pushed open the shop door and set the overhead bell tinkling, Nona, the grey haired, stooped matriarch of the Makris family, gave me a bright gummy smile of recognition. She reached for the box of cones under the counter. "Good afternoon, Katrina," she said, her dark eyes alive and twinkling and belying her grand old age of eighty nine. "How many today, dear?"

"Let's see. Four in the trailer and one in the car. That makes five scoops of vanilla today, thanks, Nona."

"And you? You like some of my Petar's home-made ice cream too? He does good job. No?"

"He does good job. *Yes!*" My taste buds already salivating at the thought of being seduced by Petar's home made recipe, I studied the twelve available flavors in the tubs on the other side of the see-through plastic screen. Petar Makris's ice-cream was the toast of the North. Absolutely mouth-wateringly yummy. The taste of the fruit dripped off the tongue as the cold confection slipped down the throat.

"Let's see," I mused and leaned closer, all the better to select a flavor. But which one? I loved them all. Blueberry? Tutti-frutti? Lemon Sherbet? Chocoholic's Delight? I shook my head. "Mrs. Makris, you can tell your son from me that he makes it almost impossible for his customers to make a decision. Doesn't matter which flavor ice cream I select, there's another eleven I've missed out on. Okay, today's choice is… Eeney, Meeney, Miney, Mo… Banana Dream."

"You make good decision, Katrina. My favorite too."

"Bet you say that to all your customers," I said and grinned. "No matter which flavor they choose."

Her toothless smile as she dug deep into the banana ice cream with her metal scoop and delivered a large portion to my cone, proved me right.

I paid, said my farewells, and juggling three ice creams precariously in each hand, turned away from the counter. Couldn't wait to see the expression of delight on the dogs' faces when I opened their trailer doors and they got an eyeful of their treat. Although to be honest, in the past, the dogs barely tasted their gourmet treat. Especially Clark. One swallow and the entire ice cream—cone and all—was no more. I wondered if dogs suffered from an ice-cream headache? If so, I wouldn't like to be in Clark's shoes. Or head afterwards.

"What that boy doing at your car?"

Nona's voice, shrill in protest, came from behind me.

"Qeek, Katrina! Dog will get loose!"

Pushing through tiredness and jumbled thoughts regarding Clark's ice cream headache, I looked through the shop window, my gaze settling on my car and trailer which I'd parked lengthwise beside the gutter in front of the shop. A tow haired boy of about eight or nine wearing khaki cargo pants, the crotch drooping around his knees, was in the act of opening the rear door of my car. Damn kid. Where was his mother?

"Hey, you! Kid! Get away from there!"

Racing from the shop to give the boy a good telling off, my mouth gaped so wide I almost swallowed a fly. The kid had a slip lead in his hand *and* he was sliding the lead over Stanley's head. What the heck was going on around here? Had someone started up a Dog-napping Class 101 at the local Community college and somehow let the instruction handbook spill into primary school curriculums around the state?

Luckily the author of the handbook had failed to write a chapter explaining the insatiable greed of some dogs on the dog-napping hit list. After licking the boy's face and preparing to jump out of the car and go for a walk with his new friend, Stanley glanced up and spotted me—or should I say the ice creams in my hands. His eyes lit up, his smile widened into the size of a ball park and with a woof of pure joy he yanked the lead from the boy's hand and zeroed in on me.

"No, Stanley! Staaaay! Siiiiit!"

Instinctively I covered my face with both ice-cream filled hands. There was no way known to man or beast that Stanley was going to stop his mad charge. And I knew it. In fact, I barely got the words out of my mouth before thirty five kilos of red brindle determined canine hurled itself at me.

My puny body didn't stand a chance. The dog's tunnel vision was programmed on one thing only—expensive gourmet ice creams.

Tongue already slurping, Stanley landed in a heap on top of me and as we both hit the pavement in a tangle of arms, legs, and paws I let out a loud *oof!* Two iced confections mashed into my face and ran down my chin onto my shirt while Stanley chased and expertly caught those that shot in the air in four different directions. A vague thought skipped through my mind as I lay flat on my back staring at the sky.

Why me? Surely this only happens to people in comic books?

Through blurred vision caused by mashed and fast-melting vanilla and banana ice-cream, I transferred my gaze to the Holden parked behind my trailer. Why did it look familiar? The windscreen was scratched and the noise and vibration from the car's exhaust had the doors rattling. And then it hit me. Bloody Purple Pants was at it again. I should have known he was behind the attempted dog-napping. Desperately, I grabbed at the dangling lead around Stanley's neck and held on.

You're not getting *this* dog, buster!

The guy most likely to be voted No. 1 in the Substandard Crook of the Year Award stuck his head through the car's open window, his leathery forehead furrowed in an angry frustrated frown. "Shut your mouth and run!" he snarled to the boy dithering beside my car and then with a clash of gears he followed his own advice and roared from the shopping center, leaving a trail of smoke in his wake.

Had PP—aka Purple Pants—been following me since I left the track? Had he noticed the red brindle dog in the back seat of my car, and, believing it was Lofty, enlisted the help of a passing kid to steal the dog?

That's it. I'd had enough. Time to show this long-in-the-tooth, ham-handed robber-in-training exactly who he was tangling with. Time *Miss Nice Girl* went out-for-lunch and my alter-ego, *Bombshell Chick* hijacked the show.

Up until now, I'd been sitting back allowing this thug to intimidate me. Trespass on my property. Steal my dogs. Hurt Stella. Well, not any more…

From now on Mr. Purple Pants was in for one heck of a fight.

6

MY KICK ASS, *Miss Bombshell Chick* persona commandeered the wheel of the car all the way home. I hung onto the steering wheel as though it might do a runner, swore at slow moving traffic and entertained myself by imagining wringing PP's scrawny neck. Very slowly. And with a beatific smile on my face.

However, after a night spent refereeing three recalcitrant greyhounds and a very snotty Chihuahua, my tough, positive facade began to wilt. So much so, when I woke the following morning—an hour after my normal six o'clock start—I was more a deflated balloon than a feisty female Tarzan.

"Get off me, you big dodo!" I shouted, shoving at the thirty five kilo dog stretched across my chest. Stanley opened one eye, then, deciding he could still manage to sleep without using me as a mattress, closed it again.

Snuggled beside me, black head sharing my pillow, Lucky gave a sharp woof to get my attention, then smiled up at me. "And *you've* got nothing to grin about, madam." I gave her a mock scowl and she replied with an even wider grin and a slurp to my nose. "Dogs who run around the house with the remote control in their mouth and turn the television on full blare at 3 am usually find themselves living back in the kennel block." I shook my head at her. Tutted. "This is *so* not like you, Lucky." More licks, this time with her head off the pillow so she could give my cheek her full treatment. "You should have shown our guests the correct way to behave inside the house—not acted like Queen of the Underbelly Gang."

Heavy-eyed, I finally dragged myself out of bed and let the Underbelly Gang into the house yard to run around and empty while I showered, dressed and cooked breakfast. Well, that's if you consider a slice of honey-smeared toast and a cup of instant coffee a cooked breakfast. It was mornings like this I wished my seven foot biker buddy, Scuzz, was still around. Or should I say the breakfast of bacon, eggs, tomato and sausages he cooked for me while he was my bodyguard, back when Tireman Pete was out to get me. It even crossed my mind to send Scuzz a text message to ask him if he was available for bodyguard duties again. I could imagine the expression on Purple Pants' face if he ever came up against seven feet of hard wired biker—he'd take one look and run screaming to his mamma.

But what about Ben? If Scuzz arrived back in my life, complete with dancing tattoos, rock hard body, soft lips and lovingly polished Harley Davidson, I'd be inviting trouble. As much as the two men in my life had finally become mates, it was a cautious friendship that blossomed only through distance. Perhaps, this time, I'd manage without the help of my biker buddy.

After calling the dogs inside and threatening to confiscate their toys if I heard one more rude word between them, I set out bowls of kibble, supervised who ate where and filled the water bucket in the laundry before heading for the kennel house.

As usual, Jake, my dude helper and I, had a busy morning planned. Youngsters to trial at a nearby breaking-in track, the four racers from yesterday to check and treat with the ultrasonic machine, plus normal training duties. So it was late morning before I finally slipped a lead over Stanley's head, conned him to jump in the car and drove to the Two Wells Veterinary Clinic.

Poor Stanley. It was as though he knew where we were heading. His head anxiously swung back and forth, eyes checking out every building we passed. No matter how I sugar-coated his coming ordeal he wasn't having a bar of it.

The waiting room at the clinic was empty, not even Val, the receptionist, was around, so I left Stanley in the car and went for a snoop around the back. And that's where I found Dr. Terry Blackburn, our beloved local vet, in a small paddock adjoining his surgery. He was kneeling on the ground, both sleeves of his stained white coat rolled past his elbows, unmentionable brown stuff covering one bare arm and the other shoulder deep inside a cow's *whatsit*.

Yuck! "What are you doing?"

"Hi, Kat," Terry said, his hundred megawatt smile making me reach for my sunglasses while the sight of him stuffing intestines back into an indisposed cow had my stomach threatening to hurl. "You've caught me in the middle of attempting to restore all Bessie's bits and bobs. Poor girl aborted her calf."

My face must have gone white. Or perhaps Terry didn't want me fainting and distracting him from his job. He flicked his head in the direction of a bale of hay set up to keep the wind from his patient. "Why don't you sit over there and tell me what you've been up to?"

I cringed. The tiny lifeless form of a premature baby calf lay slumped against the hay bale.

"Terry," I said, striving to keep the horror out of my voice. "Can you *really* fit all that stuff back inside? There's so much of it. Aren't you afraid you'll forget to put an important bit back in? "

From his unenviable position at ground level, getting an eyeful of the cow's interior, he let out a loud guffaw. "Not really. Even as a kid I was pretty good at jigsaw puzzles."

I watched him strain every muscle to reach further inside the cow's *whatsit*. And just when I was contemplating leaning forward to grab the man's legs before he disappeared completely—never to be seen again— Dr. Terry Blackburn rocked backwards and his right arm slipped out of the cow with a resounding slurp.

For a moment he sat back on his heels and surveyed the mile and a half of intestines still decorating the ground. Finally, looking up, he graced me with another of his beatific smiles.

"Kat...darling. I really need you to give me a hand here."

My mouth shot open in the proverbial fly-catching position. Who me? Help with *that*? I grabbed a quick breath, took an instinctive step back and stared bug-eyed at the slimy entrails hanging from the back of the cow. "Umm…well, I'm only here to drop Stanley off…"

"Pretty please?" Terry linked his latex gloved fingers together in a begging position. "My assistant is in surgery repairing a broken hock on a Doberman and Val, our receptionist, is having a tooth filled at the dentist." He fluttered his eyelashes. They were long and thick and if they were mine I guess I'd use them for seduction too. "I'll shout you a king-sized T-bone at the new Steak-House that opened in Virginia last month."

"I-I'm not really into steak." Especially with cow's intestines spread out like alien slime at my feet.

"Come on, Kat…without your help Bessie could die."

"That's blackmail, Terry, and you know it."

"All's fair in love and saving my patient."

I glanced down at my white jeans and pale green tank top. Clothes I'd donned to meet Tanya at the Mall, where we planned to discuss 'Plan A' during her lunch break. Paul Simmons, Tanya's once-again-smitten, policeman boyfriend had reluctantly given her the address of Purple Pants—known on his car registration papers as Jack Lantana. Paul warned us to keep our noses out and leave it to him to follow through, but we knew there was little he could do—Jack Lantana didn't actually *have* any of my dogs in his possession—hence the need for Plan A. We figured a little nosing around on Jack's property, preferably when he wasn't there, might unearth some answers to my baffling question: Why did he want to steal my dogs?

"Kat?"

I quickly shoved the Jack Lantana problem to one side for later so I could stare down at my current dilemma. And shudder. Yep. It was still there in all its Technicolor glory. The cow—the blood and guts—and the dirt.

There was no way out, so I let out a sigh and hoisted the white flag. "I know I'm going to regret this Terry, but what do you want me to do?"

"Good girl. Now, don't worry about your clothes, there's a white coat on the front seat of my four-wheel drive. Put that on then refill this metal bucket with hot water. And if you grab a clean cake of soap from the second drawer in the cupboard just inside the surgery door, I'll love you forever and name my first child after you."

I grinned at his effusiveness. Couldn't help it. Terry Blackburn was one of those rare guys you couldn't take offense with. "Talking of love…and children," I purred. "How's that gorgeous fiancé of yours? Either of you decided on a day to tie the knot yet or are you aiming for a mention in the World Guinness book of Records as the couple with the longest engagement?"

"What's this, Kat? Trying to marry me off?" His smile broadened. "And here I was thinking you wanted me for yourself." On his knees, he shifted position and I couldn't help admiring his fit thighs. Evidently veterinary work was as good for the body as an active membership at the local gym. "Although I heard you finally collared that arrogant so and so, Ben Taylor."

I quickly took my eyes away from forbidden territory and matched his grin. "Yep. You heard right. Ben and I are now an item."

"Hmm… Ben always did have good taste. Only ever played with the pretty ones."

"Played with the pretty ones—and settled for me."

Terry nodded then turned away but not before I saw the smile slide off his face. Was he trying to warn me off Ben? I stared at the tension across his back as he ran a hand over Bessie's rump. No, I was reading things into the conversation that weren't there. Okay, until recently Ben had worn a new girl on his arm every week but since we'd been together he was definitely monogamous. Or was he? I shook my head. Thought back to yesterday when we'd laughed and cuddled as we poured over the illustrations in the *Kama Sutra*. Of course he was. Not only were we lovers we were also good mates.

Plus I'd kill him if he so much as glanced at another woman.

Too happy with our new relationship to let any rain clouds darken my sky, I dropped my tote bag on the bale of hay and straightened my top. "Don't worry, Terry, that's all in the past. Now, I'll go get that hot water for you."

A few minutes later, swamped by a white coat three sizes too big, I staggered through the paddock gate, a bucket of hot water in one hand and a bar of soap in the other.

Terry, deep inside the cow again, glanced up as I placed the bucket beside him. "Thanks Kat, now toss me the beer bottle from inside my bag."

"You're taking time out for a beer? What about Bessie?"

The twinkle in Terry's eyes could have lit up the sky on a moonless night. "Not that I'd say no to a nice cold beer, darlin', but the bottle in my bag is empty."

I frowned as I unearthed the bottle and brandished it in the air. "Now what?"

"Wash it thoroughly, using plenty of soap. What's going on here is I'm having trouble reaching far enough inside the cow and sometimes a bottle gives me that extra reach. Always worth a try."

And here was I believing science had zinged into the twenty first century with a burst of fanfare and musical commercials on television.

By the time Terry had returned everything to its rightful place and followed this procedure with a liberal dose of antibiotic powder, I felt like I knew the insides of a cow rather intimately. Especially after he persuaded me to insert my arm in the narrow passage and hold the bottle in place while he raced inside the surgery for a syringe and follow-up antibiotic injection.

What poor Bessie must have been going through during all this pain and indignity, I could only imagine. Or on second thoughts—holy catfish—no, I couldn't.

After binning our coats in a laundry chute, we scrubbed up in the little bathroom set off from the surgery.

"Thanks, Kat. You're a star." Terry gave me a breath-robbing bear hug. A breath-robbing *brotherly* bear hug. "And remember, if you're ever looking for a new job, there's always one here with me."

"Hmmm…I might give that opportunity a miss." I gave an exaggerated shudder. "After today's experience I don't think I'll *ever* eat tripe or brains or even spaghetti again."

Big and cuddly and constantly smiling, Dr. Terry Blackburn had the heart of a marshmallow and I often wondered how he'd ever decided on the career of a veterinarian. Losing animals he vowed to save was always a major disaster for him. In fact, if it wasn't for Terry, the Greyhound Adoption Program would have been in financial trouble. As the GAP's official vet, Terry gave his services to the program for the cost of medications only, claiming it was his contribution to the recycling of greyhounds from racing dogs to lounge-lizards.

After transferring a nervous Stanley from the car to an empty kennel in the animal hospital, I popped my head into the surgery to take my leave. Terry was at his desk entering Bessie's details into the computer.

"Okay if I pick Stanley up in the morning?" I asked, refusing to let the dismal howls of protest emerging from behind the closed door of the hospital affect me.

Terry looked up and nodded.

"Sorry about the noise. I did try to reassure him but I think it might have been the word 'snip' that put him off."

"Snip? No, no, no. Katrina, that's not a word you use lightly around males." And then he let out a chuckle. "Don't worry, Stanley will be fine. By the way, how's his sister doing? Stitches okay?"

I could feel my inner *Bombshell Chick* bubbling to the surface again and checked the growl before it tore out of my throat. Not Terry's fault. All my anger was directed at the sneaky guy in purple pants. "As a matter of fact," I told him, "Stella's not okay."

"Why? What happened?"

"Some weirdo kidnapped her from her kennel, then brought her back a few minutes later and tossed her over my front fence."

Terry's face blackened into a thundercloud at my words. He pushed himself up from the computer so quickly, his chair almost toppled over. "He did *what*?"

"Threw Stella over my fence." I closed my hands into fists until my fingernails dug into the palms. "And the fall tore out three of her stitches."

"Bastard." He shook his head, concern etched on his face. "Do you want me to drop in later this afternoon and stitch her up again?"

"You're a sweetie, but no thanks. I've cleaned the wound and she's now a guest inside my house. Although there was a little friction last night with the introduction of *two* new guests, Uncle Tater and Aunty Lucky have promised to look after Stella." I made my way to the door but stopped, my fingers embracing the doorknob. "You know what? Tanya and I figure the thief might have grabbed the wrong dog."

"I don't understand."

"Well, doesn't it seem weird the guy brought Stella back so quickly and dumped her over the fence like trash?" I tramped back to the desk and leant both hands on the cluttered surface. Mind ticking over like an unexploded bomb. "Maybe, as well as color blind and thinking he looks cool in bright purple pants topped with a Hawaiian shirt, the man's gender blind too. Maybe he mistook Stella for Lofty."

"Bit of a stretch."

"Yeah, but Lofty *is* the same brindle color as Stella."

"And about fifteen kilos heavier."

It was like I had this thick rubber band circling my head and with every *maybe* the band tightened. I sank into the wooden backed chair in front of Terry's desk and rubbed my throbbing temples with the tips of my fingers. Any minute now the unexploded bomb in my head would go Kaboom.

Yet I still felt I was on the right track.

I picked up a biro and twirled it in my fingers. "When I was driving back from the track yesterday, the same guy attempted to nick Stanley."

Terry's mouth opened but no sound came out.

"But Stanley was more interested in guzzling ice-cream than being nabbed, so the piece-of-scum thief drove off empty handed."

"*Now* you're making sense. Stanley *could* be mistaken for Lofty by those who aren't acquainted with Lofty's...shall we be kind and say...*distinctive* features."

"Yes, *distinctive* sounds so much nicer than *pit-bull ugly*. Only thing is," I continued, thinking aloud, "I can't figure out why the thief would risk being caught and charged for stealing *any* of my dogs. There's no way he can sell or race them, I'd still have the registration papers. And the grader at every track would be alerted to keep an eye out for any suspicious nominations."

Terry tapped the last of Bessie's details into his computer and stood up. "Okay, what do you know about this guy?"

"Not a thing! I've never seen the jerk before and haven't a clue why he's interested in my dogs." I lifted one shoulder in a mystified shrug, then frowned. "But hey, that will change once Tanya and I put our heads together and get *Plan A* up and going. A policeman friend has been coerced into following up on the rego number of the car and he's given us an address—so very soon we'll be paying Mr. Purple Pants a visit."

"Is it wise to go see him though, Kat?" The worry lines between Terry's eyes deepened. "The man could be dangerous."

I shrugged one shoulder. Dangerous? Hell, the way I felt, Tanya and I could take the old guy out by sneezing on him. As long as we confiscated his brass knuckle duster first. "No worries, I'll have Tanya with me." I sent Terry a knowing wink and stood up ready to leave. I was running late and my friend would be waiting for me at the mall. "The way her hormones are swinging at the moment, if the man so much as raises a finger, she'll flatten him with the nearest heavy duty frypan."

Terry laughed, flashing irresistible dimples. "Guess that explains why I saw her chasing her ex out the front door with a broom when I drove past her property last week."

"Not necessarily." I turned at the door, grinned and spoke over my shoulder before hurrying off to meet my hormonal friend. "Dan more than likely lost Tanya's maintenance money on the favorite in the last race at Globe Derby—and then had the gall to ask her for a loan."

7

It was nine hours later. On a night when the moon wasn't home and dark rain clouds threatened to gobble up the few stray stars.

While Tanya carefully aligned her little red car beside the gutter in front of a house direct from a Hitchcock movie, I tugged the collar of my sheepskin coat up around my ears and slunk further down into the passenger seat.

Maybe the plan we'd come up with over warm chicken salad at the Café Aqua wasn't such a good idea. Quite doable in the middle of the day while surrounded by chattering, laughing diners—but on a lonely road in the middle of the night—I was having second and even third thoughts.

On the condition Tanya would accept a dinner date with Policeman Paul, a condition which didn't seem to displease her, in fact she'd been all smiley and gung ho when she'd imparted her new-found knowledge at the mall earlier today—Paul had infiltrated the Car Registry data base and come up with a name for the owner of the pus colored Holden:

Jack Aloysius Lantana.

And at this very moment we were camped outside his house.

I squinted at the shadowy property illuminated by a lone flashing street lamp. "Guess we'll have to come back tomorrow. Lantana's either asleep or gone out."

Tanya, eyes fixed on the dark windows of the house, switched off the engine and pocketed her car keys. "I suppose we *could* hang a left here tomorrow and question the guy," she drawled. "But, don't you think this would be a good opportunity to case the joint?"

"Case the joint?" I laughed at my friend's choice of words. "Where'd you pick up that terminology? Sounds like you've been reading murder mysteries instead of your usual happy-ever-after romance novels."

Tanya rolled her eyes and muscled the car door open against the strengthening wind. "Where's your investigative spirit, Kat?"

Good question. I shivered when a peppercorn tree looming overhead whipped and twisted—its low branches scraping warning fingers across the roof of the car. It was a wind similar to the night I trusted Peter Manning. The night I barely survived my last investigation. The night I almost ended up as ash on the floor of Manning's Crematorium.

"My investigative spirit?" I repeated and sank further into the sanctuary of the warm sheepskin covered seat. "Probably hiding under a pile of discarded socks at the bottom of my closet."

Insensitive to my concerns, Tanya ploughed onwards. "I thought you *wanted* to know why this piece-of-shit was stealing your dogs?"

I sighed. Grabbed a mental shovel and buried my fears in a shallow grave where I could quickly unearth them if necessary. "Of course I do, Tan. Here I am being weak-bellied and pathetic—a soggy pool of watery custard—while you're ready to bust down doors to find the truth. You're right. My dogs are at risk and I don't know why. The creep who lives in this house *does*." I flashed her a grin. "So, let's say we go pound some answers out of Mr. Jack Aloysius Lantana."

I joined Tanya on the footpath, flashlight at the ready. Yep. Time to bring my gum boots out of retirement, dust down my trench coat and slip into sleuthing mode—before this incompetent thief managed to actually steal the right dog.

However, Nancy Drew was short-lived. As though conspiring against us, the flashing street light in front of Lantana's house gave a final flicker and kicked the bucket. Suddenly, I wanted to go home. Instead, I fumbled a flashlight from my coat pocket and let its beam spill across the ground in front of us. Over an acre of overgrown land and a graveyard of rusted car bodies which seemed to be keeping vigil on either side of a dirt baked pathway snaking up to Lantana's front veranda.

With a firm shove Tanya opened the heavy wire-mesh front gate, undeterred by the scratchy squeal of unoiled hinges. "So, do we stick to our plan?"

"To the letter," I told her. "If Jack Lantana's home we ask questions, perhaps threaten him with the police. If he's not home, we take a quick peep through the windows and then leave. No skulking around his garage or outbuildings. Okay? That's called *trespassing!*" Plus poking around amongst rats and spiders and other creepy crawlies in the dark—discovering god knows what—wasn't my idea of a fun night out.

Tanya didn't answer. And that always made me nervous.

Half-way along the dirt path I could feel the glassless windows of the hunkering car bodies, like eyes, following our every step. Ahead, radiating menace, the sprawling farmhouse reared out of the darkness.

What the hell were we doing?

My Adidas sneakers slowed down and came to a faltering stop. "I don't know about you, Tan," I whispered, throat dry and uncooperative, "but my gut's telling me to high-tail it out of here. Fast. In fact, it's screaming at me to come back tomorrow…in the daylight."

Tanya, who was so close she kept banging shoulders with me, slipped an arm through mine and continued walking. "Come on, Kat, we can't chicken out now. It's common knowledge that all successful detectives do their detecting in the hours of darkness."

My snigger broke through the heavy silence. "Says who?"

"Well…" Tanya paused but didn't stop walking. "Kinsey Millhone doesn't investigate a suspect in the noon-day sun, does she? And look how successful she is."

"She might be successful, but she's also *not real*. Kinsey Millhone is a figment of Sue Grafton's imagination—a character from a book."

The nearer we drew to the house, the more I wanted to put on my brakes. Turn tail and skedaddle back to the car. Go home. The thought of sharing a family sized pizza with Tater and Lucky and our two canine guests, Stella and Stanley, all of us zoned out in front of the television, seemed a much more sensible alternative to what I was doing right now. I sighed. Where had my brain been hiding when I'd let my hormonal, gung-ho friend talk me into paying our geriatric dog-napper a visit in the middle of the night?

Unease, with all its shivery manifestations, continued to bite at my gut as we neared the four rickety steps leading up onto the overhanging front veranda. Who knew what lay beyond that front door? Jack Lantana, dressed in psychedelic orange and yellow pajamas, leering manically at us while sharpening his axe to a fine edge on wet sandstone?

Beside me, Tanya inhaled a deep breath. "You know what, Kat, I think—"

I never did get to hear what Tanya thought.

From the bowels of the closest wreck, a rusted-out car body that looked like it had been propped up on blocks for the last fifty odd years, slunk two dark creatures of the night.

Guard dogs…

Or to be more precise—large, slit-eyed, black and tan Rottweilers, their fierce growls indicating they were ready to tear out throats and swallow human tonsils.

A harsh panting noise pounded in my ears. I didn't know if it came from Tanya, the dogs or me. A sour urine-like stench assailed my nostrils. Once again, I didn't know if it came from Tanya, the dogs or me…

Then, like a well-oiled team, the two dogs slunk in behind us and posed; bodies' rigid, snarls vowing menace.

Holy catfish!

I clutched at my throat which suddenly felt very exposed, very vulnerable. Retreat would now result in copious blood, a plethora of screams and definite hospitalization—or worse. Hand trembling, I shone the flashlight on our aggressors and my heart did a painful belly-flop. Every hair along the dogs' backs stood on end. Their mean mouths drooled in anticipation. And the smell of hostility and old meat had my stomach heaving.

"Run!" yelled Tanya.

As if I needed any prodding…

All systems struggling to suck more blood and air and speed from my deeply traumatized body, I flew up the steps onto the veranda where Tanya was already hurling her shoulder against the front door.

"Is it lock–?" A sharp pain turned my words into a piercing scream. Almost brought me to my knees. The leading Rottweiler, the one with the white foam spewing like shaving cream from his mouth, had latched onto the seat of my jeans.

I was going to die. Ripped to shreds by a crazy demented canine. I must have done something horrendous in a previous life to deserve to die like this.

It was so unfair—I was a lover of dogs.

"Quick, Kat…in here!"

Before Cujo could spit out the jagged piece of denim and sink his fangs into exposed flesh, I fell through the open doorway into Tanya's waiting arms.

Between us, we managed to slam and bolt the door from the inside, catching Rottweiler number one's nose in the act. A chilling howl preceded by a crashing thump shook the door on its hinges and rattled crockery half a block away.

Tanya grabbed my arm and hung on like it was the last pair of Jimmy Choos on the sales counter. "You okay, Kat?"

With no breath left to do anything else, I nodded.

In the mad rush for the door I'd dropped my flashlight, probably glowing inside one of the Cujo's stomachs by now, and in the stifling darkness I could barely see Tanya's shadowy figure. It was bad enough we were trespassing in Jack Lantana's house. It was bad enough we had no way of getting out without being eaten. But I was damn sure I wasn't going to stand here shivering and gasping in the dark one moment longer. Chest wheezing, bum on fire, I pried Tanya's claw-like fingers one by one from my arm and searched for the light switch.

Eyes huge in her pale face, Tanya stared back at me. "Shit!" she breathed, blinking in the sudden light. "That was close!"

Tanya Ashton: the master of understatement.

The tuna patties I'd eaten for dinner warred with nerves so tightly strained I wouldn't be surprised if they unraveled and left me limper than a rag doll. Shaking, I burrowed my fingers into my back pocket and pulled out my mobile. "I'm going to ring Ben."

"Not a good idea," advised Tanya with a small shake of her head. "Ben thinks he's indestructible. Tell him we're in trouble and he'll come galloping over here like a knight in shining armor instead of torn jeans and checked flannel shirt. And what do you reckon the guard dogs will do to him? Lick his face and play ball? I don't think so."

She was right. Cujo1 and Cujo2 would turn Ben into chopped liver and then spit out the bones. We needed plan B. I rammed my mobile into my pocket and tore at a hang nail with my teeth. "If we had some juicy lamb chops we could toss them through one of the back windows and escape while the dogs were eating."

"Wouldn't work. We'd need to empty a butcher shop to keep those two eating long enough for us to reach the front gate."

"Well, do *you* have a better idea?"

"How about we shoot 'em?"

I blinked. Gave her a *duh* look. "Shoot them with what? A slingshot made out of knicker elastic and a bag of frozen peas as ammunition?"

"Sorry." Clearly on edge, Tanya threw back her head and let out a pent up breath. "I'm nervous. I can't think straight when I'm nervous." She raked both hands through her hair which made it stand on end. "I need alcohol."

"Alcohol? Tanya, this isn't a hotel."

"No worries, I'll go check out Lantana's fridge, see if he's got any booze, and while I'm there, with any luck, I'll find a couple of sheep for the dogs stashed in the meat container."

Another crashing thump shook the front door. My heart, already stressed to the max gave a plaintive bleat and attempted to batter its way out of my chest.

Tanya, who hadn't felt the deadly scrape of canine teeth on her backside, merely scowled at the door then picked up and brandished a big ugly statue of what looked like an overweight vampire with bloodshot eyes. When the door stopped shaking she placed her weapon back on the hall stand and shrugged. "At least we don't have to worry about Jack Lantana popping out of his bedroom. He's definitely not home. Only the dead could sleep through that noise." She swiveled on one foot and set off down the passageway. "Which means we only have the dogs to worry about—unless, of course, Lantana shows up and finds us stuck in here."

I set up a mental force field and refused to allow her last throwaway comment to filter into my already overtaxed brain.

While my PMT affected friend went hunting for booze and red meat, I decided to have a quick snoop around. Okay, I was no Kinsey Millhone and never would be, but who knows… I might be lucky enough to fall over a clue that explained why Lantana was so dead keen on stealing my dogs.

The first room I came to appeared to be set up as a study or an office. The desktop computer was turned on, and a colorful screensaver featuring a dancing naked woman with breasts the size of basketball hoops provided the entertainment. Newspapers, greyhound racing magazines and betting guides covered every available space on the desk and spilled over onto the floor. Desk drawers lay open and the contents scattered across the room. Books dragged from shelves littered the carpet.

What a mess! I didn't have to be a detective, fictional or real, to realize either Lantana was the world's worst housekeeper or he'd had a visit from an intruder. Even Linus from the Charlie Brown comics could work that one out. Questions crowded my mind. Why would an intruder break into Lantana's house? And did they find what they'd been searching for? And the Million Dollar Question–*how did the intruder manage to get past the dogs without losing at least one limb?*

And then another big fat ugly thought hit me.

Tanya and I were inside the burgled house. If anything was missing, guess who'd get the blame? And unless Tanya found some munchies for the dogs pretty damn quick, we'd be sitting here twiddling our thumbs when the owner of the house arrived home and rang the police.

Caught between the desire to poke through papers on the floor and fear of being charged with break-and-entry, I hovered a few feet inside the doorway. It wouldn't do to leave my fingerprints on anything. Especially as my fingerprints were now on the database down at the local police station.

I let out a sigh of frustration and shook my head. Yep, I'd be better off helping Tanya distract the dogs so we could get the hell out of here.

As I turned to leave, a glint of deep red on the desk beside the computer caught my eye. I took a step closer. No, it couldn't be. Surely that wasn't the bracelet from the set Dad gave my sister, Liz, for her fourteenth birthday? The ruby bracelet that matched the necklace Liz left behind for me when she ran away from home?

Fingering the familiar necklace at my throat, I glanced up and down the passageway, noted it was currently empty, so scurried across to the desk. And, hand hovering over the piece of jewelry, I paused to reconsider. Did I really want to know if the bracelet was Liz's? If so— what would that imply? It couldn't bear thinking of for it would mean Liz and Lantana knew each other. Which didn't make sense. Mind swirling, I scooped the bracelet up and turned it over. Yep. There on the back next to the gold clasp were the same initials engraved on the underside of my necklace—*E.J.M.*

Elizabeth Jennifer McKinley.

A shiver, colder than a blast of wind blowing across the icy stretches of Antarctica set my teeth chattering. What was Liz's bracelet doing on Jack Lantana's desk? Had she been in this house for some reason and left her bracelet behind? Or was there something more sinister going on? Did it have anything to do with her moving on, disappearing, and leaving Scott, her boyfriend, behind?

Still shivering, I swallowed the lump in my throat, slipped the ruby bracelet onto my wrist in case the police found us here and leaned forward to get a closer look at a small block of yellow post-it notes lying beside the phone. The top sheet had indentations from the last reminder Jack had written to himself. A phone number? A helpful name? A clue linking Lantana with my sister, Liz? If I tore off the top page I'd leave my fingerprints behind. Not a good idea. Instead, I slipped the whole block of yellow post-its into my pocket and turned my attention to the flashing computer. Now, if only I could move that damn screensaver without leaving fingerprints and get a look at what Lantana had been working on…

Both hands clasped firmly behind my back so there'd be no chance of accidentally losing a print I nudged the mouse with my hip. Immediately, the dancing nude disappeared from the screen and in her place was a web page, downloaded from a greyhound breeding program. What dog was Lantana interested in? I bent forward to study the particulars and almost wet my pants when a blood-curdling scream sent my heart into free fall.

Something bad had happened to Tanya.

"Hang on, I'm coming!"

Another scream, even more terrified than the first, directed me to the back of the house where I found Tanya in a rundown kitchen that looked like it was set in a 1950s time warp, green laminated table top, old style kitchen hatch, worn linoleum floor covering.

"What is it, Tan? What's happened?"

Tanya stared at me, her eyes wide and bulging. Then, one hand covering her mouth, she slowly lifted her other arm, and pointed at the open refrigerator. I followed her shaking finger and felt the room spin.

Tanya hadn't found meat for the dogs. Or booze. Bathed by the inside door light of the refrigerator I could see all the wire shelves had been removed and Jack Lantana had been jammed in, knees scrunched under his chin, arms wrapped around his scrawny bare chicken legs. Not only had his purple pants been removed—he had died the way he'd been born. Completely naked. After gaping for what felt like a hundred years at his poor shriveled penis, my eyes shifted up over the soft paunch and the sunken chest to his head. A wrecked head. A head that had been beaten out of shape by something hard, blunt, and deadly.

And I knew, without going any closer, that Jack Lantana would never steal another dog.

8

Whoever stashed Jack in the refrigerator must have turned the gauge to minus 50 degrees. Ice clung to his broken nose, his bloodied lifeless eyes were frozen popsicles and if I leant forward and gave his ear a tug I had a feeling it would break off in my hand. Even the blood from his smashed skull was no longer liquid. Blood that had spurted, congealed or spilled down onto his nakedness, now resembled paint from a child's finger painting.

I wanted to be sick. I wanted to scream. I wanted to slam the refrigerator door shut and block the sight of dead Jack from view, but my feet refused to take me closer to the nightmare. Instead, they turned into two lead weights and became rooted to the spot. I still hadn't recovered from waking beside my first dead body six weeks ago and here I was in the presence of another one.

A nervous lump clogged my throat and with an effort I tore my eyes away from the *thing* in the refrigerator, the *thing* that used to be Jack Lantana, and turned towards Tanya. In the dim light from the fly-spotted bulb in the kitchen, I could see my white faced friend clutching at a wooden rail-backed chair for support.

"Jesus!" She finally gasped, her breath wheezing like she'd just crossed the finish line in a Bay to City marathon. "Is that—"

Almost choking, I swallowed the lump in my throat before answering. "Tanya, meet my dog-napper. Jack Lantana."

"He looks so…so…"

"Dead?"

"And…so meaty. You know, like a…a butcher shop."

Tanya was right. From this day forth, the nauseating stench of blood and the image of Jack Lantana's raw gaping head would precede me every time I set foot in a butcher's shop. I was just contemplating the pros and cons of turning vegetarian, when Tanya spun around and took off out of the kitchen like she'd been bitten by a swarm of bees.

I followed her. No way did I want to be left alone with *that*. What if, now the refrigerator door was open, Jack started to melt? Would the blood melt too? Would the blood trickle out in a pool over the gray linoleum? I started to run. No way did I want to hang around in front of the refrigerator and risk drowning in melting blood.

"I've gotta find something to drink," Tanya called over her shoulder as she made a dash down the passageway and into the first room on the left which was Jack's lounge room. "And I don't mean water."

"Shouldn't we ring the police first?" I asked, then froze–half-in, half-out of the doorway. An upturned coffee table, now minus one leg, shards of opaque glass with the remains of what looked like a cheap vase, and dirty white lace curtains torn from a smashed window littered the stained carpet. Clearly Jack had put up one heck of a fight. But the ugly stain, dark red against a pale green background, showed the exact spot where he'd fought and lost.

Oh God. I really didn't want to be here. If only I could go home, lock all the doors, take a cleansing shower, slip into my comfortable Pooh Bear nightdress and watch an old romance movie on Channel 72, squashed up on the sofa with my dogs.

"Kat, you're not thinking straight," said Tanya. "Look around. We're not in a public place here. It's not the Mall or the cinema or the greyhound track. We're trespassing in the dead guy's house." She shook her head at me as though talking to a simpleton, then punched the air when she spotted an old fashioned vinyl covered bar attached to the back wall of the room. "Believe me—this won't look good to the men in blue."

I drew in a breath and closed my eyes.

Won't look good? Hell, they'd lock us up and toss the key into the nearest crocodile infested swamp.

"I know, but we still have to ring the police," I said and grabbed a breath. "We can't get past the Cujos without their help?"

Tanya considered my latest comment while checking out the contents of the bar and the frown between her eyes deepened. Then she shrugged, reached out and snagged a slab of VB beer. "Okay," she said, tugging at the ring on one of the cans. "You make the phone call. I'll drink the booze."

After dialing 911 and admitting to Detective Inspector Adams that yes, there was another dead body and yes, I was currently in the house *with* said dead body, I wandered back into the lounge.

Already Tanya was downing her second can of VB. "Here, take this, it's all I can find. No whisky. No vodka. No wine. This guy has absolutely no taste in liquor," she said tossing me an unopened can from the slab she'd set down on the coffee table.

"We can't drink Lantana's beer. That's stealing."

"Hey, Lantana has no need for it. Where he's gone he'll be too busy dodging fire and pitchforks."

I placed the can back down on the table and studied Tanya's face. It was like last time when I'd called her after discovering Matthew Turner, a fellow greyhound trainer and a one-night-stand who'd been murdered in my bed. Tanya had hurried over to support me and ended up drunk and disorderly by the time the police arrived.

"Go easy on the alcohol," I warned her. "You know what drinking too quickly does to you, Tan."

She lifted both eyebrows at me in query.

"It turns you into a legless drunk." I threw myself down on the nearest lounge chair and sank my head in my hands. "Oh God, this looks bad for us, doesn't it?"

"Don't worry." Tanya drained her second can and immediately tore the ring off the next. "When the police see the dead guy they'll know it wasn't us. That guy's an ice block. He's been dead for hours. We've been in the house, like, ten minutes. All they'll do is ask us a couple of questions and then let us go."

I hung onto that thought. Bathed in it. Licked it up and let it warm my cold insides. As soon as Detective Adams pulled up out the front, I could walk away from this nightmare and let him take over. Let him bring in the dog-catchers. Deal with the suspicious death. Contact the coroner. Seal off the area. Turn off the fridge. And whatever else the policeman in charge did in the presence of a dead body. He was more than welcome to it.

All I wanted to do was go home.

9

So much for going home…

The basic wooden bench, splintered from years of crudely written messages, jabbed like a branding iron into the soft flesh at the back of my legs. Squirming offered no relief. I slid a furtive glance to the metal bunks cemented into the wall at the rear of the cell. Flinched at the sight of thin unwelcome mattresses, even thinner blankets and the lip curling scent of eau-de-urine emanating from one of its snoring occupants. And when a six foot transvestite, decked out in an iridescent green and purple mini-dress that showcased his hairy legs and frilly knickers, leaned over and burped his vomit-enhanced breath in my face—I decided I might as well bang my head against the prison bars until I passed out.

Reporting Jack Lantana's murder to Detective Inspector Adams was a big mistake. Think Tyrannosaurus Rex big. I should have contacted a nice polite uniformed constable and left the Colombo look-alike to get on with whatever he'd been doing before I disturbed him. Probably torturing some sweet old Granny he'd caught smoking pot to relieve the pain of her arthritis.

It took four rangers from the local dog-pound, each armed with a tranquilizer gun, to capture and remove the Cujos. But the moment they'd settled the dogs in the RSPCA vehicle, DI Adams acted. Through the smashed window of the lounge we heard Adams shouting instructions to his back-up team before hauling off and breaking down the front door.

"We must stop meeting like this," Tanya told him, saluting his hurried arrival with a can of VB beer—her sixth—as we met him on the other side of the broken door. He scowled, pushed past us and stomped toward the kitchen. We followed. When he reached the industrial sized refrigerator his face grew grim. One look inside and Adams promptly radioed in something called a Code 503: '*White Caucasian—60 to 65 years of age—around 85 kilos—probable cause of death, several blows to the head with a blunt instrument.*'

Within minutes, a team of CIB detectives and uniformed police arrived on the scene. While they spread their tentacles into every crack of Lantana's house, DI Adams produced two sets of police-issue handcuffs and, reading us our rights, fastened them around our wrists.

End result—after an hour long interrogation, Tanya and I were incarcerated in a holding cell at our local police station, awaiting bail.

I cringed as Burping Bertha belched in my face again. My stomach did a back flip and I instinctively screwed my nose and turned my head away. That's when Bertha's mate, a short fat guy with a small hairy patch just below his bottom lip and tats decorating every exposed body part, shadow-boxed in front of me—all the better to display his flopping belly and active tattoos. That was okay until he leaned into me, face so close his broken nose almost touched mine.

"Reckon ya too good for me and me mate, eh?" Tat Guy said, thin lips twisting in a sneer. "Think ya somethin' special, hey, bitch?"

I was dead meat. No—I was maggoty dead meat. I flattened my shoulders against the rough gray wall behind me until every crevice poked through my sweater. A doomed fly eying a raised can of Mortein spray.

"Oh, no," I squeaked. "Not me. I'm definitely not special. I'm just an un-special nobody."

Tat Guy made a noise like a constipated vacuum cleaner and spat on the floor, barely missing my one hundred dollar Adidas sneakers, bought at a 50% off sale. "Because if ya do, bitch, I'll have to smash ya teeth through the back of ya head." He grabbed me by the neck of my sweater. "Unnerstand?"

"Understand? Oh, yes. I understand," I gasped through partially closed off airways. "This un-special nobody understands perfectly."

Tanya, who'd been slumped on the bench beside me, singing something from West Side Story and hiccupping when she forgot the words, staggered to her feet. "Hey, you! Porky! Leave my best friend alone." Bottom lip protruding, she shoved Tat Guy in the chest, her ten pretty pink lacquered nails digging into his sweaty exposed skin.

Holy catfish! What was Tanya doing? Committing suicide? Had sculling six cans of booze in ten minutes robbed her of all rational thought?

I took a shuddering breath as Tat Guy's hold on my sweater loosened. And just when I'd resolved to break free and insert myself between Tanya and the two hundred pound porker, endure the punch that was surely coming her way, Burping Bertha reached out, his ham sized fist closing gently around Tanya's small hands. "*Dahling*," Bertha gushed. "You *have* to tell me the name of your nail polish. It's *deevine*. Where did you get it?"

Tanya stopped in mid shove. "Oh this?" she said admiring her nails like a princess admiring the Crown Jewels. "This is *Honeymoon Orgasm* in hot-pink. You can pick it up from our Virginia store, *The Luv Bug*. It's on sale this week for $8.99 a bottle."

"You work at *The Luv Bug*?" Bertha's big, craggy, heavily made up face lit up and his voice dropped ten octaves until he sounded like a bear in man's clothing. "I thought I'd seen you somewhere before. My cousin, Louie and I go there often." Bertha turned to his cousin and casually peeled the man's fingers from the neck of my sweater, allowing air to infiltrate my lungs again. "Louie, this gorgeous gal works at *The Luv Bug*. You know, that fuck-me shop where we came across those fuck-me vibrator jock straps."

Louie grinned and I swear he'd either filed his canine teeth with a rasp or he was part Vampire. "Oooh, yeah," he drawled. "And what about that blow up doll we found there? Screamed 'er 'ead off every time we stroked 'er tits?"

"*And* the leather whip with the electrodes?"

Oh…my…God.

I slumped back onto the bench, closed my eyes and let the talk of vibrating jock straps, orgasmic blow up dolls, pink handcuffs, and battery-charged whips pass right over my head.

How did I get myself into these predicaments? Why did I keep finding dead bodies? I sighed. All I wanted from life was to train enough winners to keep the bank manager from my door, watch soppy videos on the lounge with my dogs and spend time having hot sex with Ben.

I opened my eyes and blinked. I must be hallucinating. Thinking of Ben must have magically granted my wish. For there, leaning against the wall on the other side of the bars was my *One-Phone-Call*. A flutter of pleasure at the sight of his hurriedly pulled on jeans and unbuttoned shirt made me smile. He didn't smile back. In fact the crease between his eyes told me he was not especially pleased to see me.

"Ben?"

"That's me."

Hmm…definitely pissed off.

I let out a sigh and pushed up from the hard bench. Okay, I guess when you're woken at one in the morning by an almost incoherent phone call and it's your girlfriend begging you to drive to the police station to bail her out, it's enough to make you a little testy. Probably one of those random situations not covered in the latest Dating rulebook. Especially when said incoherent girlfriend confesses she's discovered a dead body—the second in the past six weeks. Oh yeah—I forgot—and once again she's a murder suspect.

"Thanks for coming." I ran the tip of my tongue over my dry lips and swallowed. "Did I wake you, babe?"

Ben rolled his eyes then glared at Tanya who was still listing all the new products due to come into the store over the next couple of weeks. "If I can drag you and Ms. Sexpert away from your new friends," he growled, "I'm here to bail you out."

A uniformed sergeant stepped forward and after producing a long black key he called our names and opened the cell door.

Hallelujah and thank God for long black cell-door keys!

Not waiting for Tanya, I rushed at Ben and engulfed him in a hug. I was so pleased to see his familiar face I could have eaten him.

He didn't respond.

Confused, I let my arms drop to my sides and frowned. Geez, I'd hugged more receptive telegraph poles.

A tic in Ben's jaw twitched and his dark accusing eyes met mine. "We talked about this, Kat," he said, hands still clamped in his jeans pockets. "I said not to go to Lantana's house alone."

"But I didn't." I bleated.

"I said I'd come with you."

So—*that's* what was up Ben's nose. Surely he couldn't be jealous of me finding a dead body. He could take over that honor any day. "Ben, before I left I rang you at home and there was no answer."

"Well, you should—"

"*And* your mobile was switched off."

He shook his head, his expression clearly telling me what he thought of my intelligence. "So, you went anyway. And not in the daylight—oh, no—you had to go visit a potential killer at night."

"I had Tanya with me."

"Tanya?" His rolling eyes were becoming a bit of a cliché.

"And if the dogs hadn't chased us we wouldn't have gone inside." I scowled back at him.

Who'd stolen my gorgeous laid-back boyfriend and substituted this cold snarly clone? If this was how he was going to act when he was annoyed, I'd rather we'd just stayed mates. I needed a hug. A loving hug. A hug to melt the ice in my chest and chase away the nightmares.

I tried again. "Ben…it was awful. There was this dead guy and—and he was scrunched up in the refrigerator and…"

Without warning the image of Jack Lantana, head bashed until it didn't resemble a human head anymore, flashed across my eyes. I could feel a tremor starting in my legs and travelling up my body. I reached for Ben's coat sleeve and clung on to stop myself from sinking to the floor. "And—and he had ice all over him and there was blood." I closed my eyes but the picture wouldn't go away. "And the back of his head was all staved in—and I could see…"

I broke off, unable to describe the way Jack Lantana's brains, white and slimy and lifeless, poked out of his skull.

Ben's arms snaked around my body and crushed me hard up against his chest. "I'm sorry, babe. You scared me shitless. Come here." His body was warm and welcoming and when he bent and kissed me on the top of my head, I let out a sigh. "It's all over, Kat," he promised. "You're safe now."

"Sorry to get you out of bed," I mumbled into the comfort of his jacket.

He chuckled and the sound of his laugh warmed me further. "I must admit I'd rather you got me *into* bed."

I snuggled closer. Benjamin Taylor smelled of damp dogs, fresh air and sunshine on rich damp earth.

10

What a relief to be home. To be welcomed at the front door by Tater, Lucky and Stella, all vying for the first lick of whatever part of my skin they could reach. I made my way through the sea of tap dancing fur on legs, routed a jar of tiny teddy biscuits from the pantry and distributed two teddies to each open mouth. The tap dancing didn't stop so I figured if I didn't let my welcome committee into the back yard pretty damn quick, we'd be knee deep in puddles.

"No noise, mind," I warned the dogs as they fell over each other in their eagerness to rush through the open door, "or you'll set the mob off in the kennel house."

Dogs attended to, I hurried into the kitchen. After filling the electric jug I reached into the cupboard over the sink and pulled down an economy sized tin of Nescafe. Caffeine—the drug of the gods.

Without a gallon of it Tanya was likely to pass out in the next five minutes.

Although it was 2 am, a time when ghosts supposedly roam the earth—which is probably why it's also a good time to be in bed, asleep—Ben, Tanya, and I decided to talk first and sleep later. After all, it's not every day you discover a dead body, your brain gets chewed up by a clichéd *good-cop-bad-cop* routine, and you become intimate with the occupants of a police station's holding cell.

When the jug boiled I snagged a colorful Simpson's mug, the largest on my black metal cup tree, and placed it on the laminated counter top. Tanya wasn't in great shape. After drinking six cans of beer in ten minutes, in the name of stress relief—her words not mine—was it any wonder? So, to join in our conversation on any useful level she required black coffee.

A bucketful of the stuff.

Looking half his age with sleep tousled hair and hastily dragged on clothes, Ben perched on the edge of a kitchen stool. Tanya, on the other hand reminded me of what Tater dragged in after he'd been on a mouse hunt. Head in her hands and an I-don't-feel-so-good expression on her slightly green face, she slumped in a chair, woebegone and limp. She groaned. "Oh God, why do I do this to myself?"

"Beats me," I said spooning coffee and sugar into a mug. "But please, if you're going to puke, the bathroom's down the hall second on the left."

Tanya flicked me a this-is-so-not-a-joke, scowl. "I know where your damn bathroom is, Katrina."

"Uh-uh…no fighting, ladies." Ben stood up and, running a hand through his already spiky hair, turned to me. "Ready with that medication?"

"Yep. Coffee number one coming up." I snapped one hand forward like a theatre nurse assisting a doctor performing surgery. Ben wrapped his fingers around the half-filled Simpson's mug and passed it on to Tanya.

"I don't need—" The rest of Tanya's words were cut off as Ben forced the coffee to her lips.

"Better drink it, Tan," I advised her, pouring cup number two in readiness. "We need your input if we're going to work out who killed Jack Lantana."

As soon as Tanya started drinking without assistance, Ben's eyes cut to me and he shook his head. "Why the heck would we want to find out who murdered *that* thug? Your alibis for the time of the murder checked out. You're in the clear. Plus your dogs are safe now."

"But are they?" I spooned five teaspoons of sugar into Tanya's second cup of coffee. This time in a red, black and white mug that stated, *Vampires Suck*. "What if whoever killed Lantana is the brains behind the dog-napping scheme and Lantana died because he goofed twice?"

"Kat, you don't batter someone to death just because they stole the wrong dog."

"Well, why else would he be killed?"

"Because the guy was a crook and probably had enemies jumping out of the woodwork." Ben slid the empty Simpson's mug onto the sink, and with an eyebrow hitch, exchanged it for *Vampires Suck* which he passed to Tanya. "But to me, it smells more like a burglary gone wrong. Didn't you say someone ransacked Lantana's office? Well, there you go. Lantana came home, caught the burglar pinching his best china, there was a fight, and Lantana came off second best."

"Second best?" Tanya growled at Ben from behind her black coffee. "Hey, if you'd eyeballed Lantana's mangled head, you wouldn't be saying that. Rumbled burglars don't hang around long enough to do the vicious damage inflicted on that guy's skull and then haul their victim across to the refrigerator, remove the wire trays and manhandle the body into a space not meant for man or beast. No. Whoever snuffed out Jack Lantana either hated his guts or it was a retribution killing. It was not your run-of-the-mill burglar fighting to get away."

"She's got a point," I put in. "And another thing, what was Liz's bracelet doing in Lantana's office?"

Tanya slapped her empty cup into my outstretched hand and fastened her fingers around her third cup of coffee. "You know, Kat," she said, her voice pensive. "I've been thinking about that bracelet."

I glanced up, momentarily distracted from refilling *Vampires Suck*. "And what did you come up with?"

"Absolutely nothing." Tanya shrugged. "Liz is too out of it, too naive, to have any shady dealings with the likes of Lantana. Okay, she smokes pot till she's tripping with the fairies—but that'd be the extent of her criminal activities. And as for having any sort of a *relationship* with that geriatric creep. God, he's at least forty years her senior."

"That's what I figured." I let out a sigh, rubbed my tired eyes. "In fact I can't come up with one thing Liz and Jack would have in common."

"Except both having shocking tastes in fashion," Tanya muttered.

That was true. Last time I'd seen Liz she'd been dressed in what looked like a long flowing orange nightdress and a purple knitted hat with a bow that could have come straight off a teapot. I shook my head in an attempt to clear the fog of so many unanswerable questions before pushing the half-empty sugar bowl across to Tanya.

Ben unhooked a *Man at Work* mug off my cup tree. "The explanation could be as simple as Liz losing her bracelet out on the street somewhere and Jack finding it."

I screwed my nose at him. "Bit coincidental."

"It's the only solution that makes sense," he assured me while pouring himself a coffee.

Still not convinced, I chewed on my bottom lip. What were the odds of Jack Lantana, the guy who tried to steal my dogs—and for some obscure reason also got himself killed and stuffed in his refrigerator—finding a bracelet my sister Liz lost, presumably in Port Augusta?

Something like 0001%?

In need of a tissue to wipe up a dribble of coffee on the table top, I slipped my hand in my pocket. And felt a jolt when my fingers fastened around the square shape of a pad of post-it notes. "Oh, yes, I forgot to mention," I said, extricating the tissue and wiping up the drips. "I took something else from Lantana's office."

"Something else?" Tanya looked in need of sustenance to soak up the coffee so I snagged a tin of chocolate biscuits from the cupboard and dumped them in the middle of the table. She frowned. "How come you didn't mention this before?"

Was this girl for real?

"Tanya, unless you've been in a coma for the last four or five hours—we've had a few *other* things on our plate."

"Well…" Tanya gestured with a double-choc Tim Tam biscuit. "Don't just stand there looking all mysterious. Give. Tell us what you found."

"It's probably nothing, but I snitched a pad of yellow post-it notes from beside Lantana's phone. Okay, as far as I could see from a quick glance there was nothing written on the pad, but it was sitting there, staring up at me, so I slipped it in my pocket."

"As you do…"

"Waste of time, really." I shrugged one shoulder, suddenly feeling foolish. Here I was acting like an amateur sleuth when all I knew about sleuthing was what I'd read in my collection of Sue Grafton books. "I just thought…well…maybe Lantana left an impression of the last thing he wrote on the top page of the pad. And—" I could feel heat rising from my neck and spreading across my face "—and it could be a clue."

Ben draped one arm across my shoulders and tugging me closer, kissed my hot cheek. "Well then Ms. McKinley, amateur detective, let's see what you got." Eyes twinkling, a grin spread across his face. "What say I buy you a detective's slouch coat for Valentine's Day, babe? Reckon you'd look good in one of those." His grin turned wicked. "Especially if you wore nothing underneath."

"Please," Tanya wailed, rolling her eyes. "If you two are going to get horny leave the room. Otherwise, can we get on with the reason we're here."

"Sorry," said Ben who didn't look at all apologetic.

I dragged my eyes away from smoldering temptation and gulped a breath of air. "Of course, if we were fictional characters, we'd find the name and address of the guy who killed Lantana imprinted on the notepad."

Tanya growled. "Would you shut up already and show us what you got."

I dragged the pad, now slightly dog-eared, from my pocket and placed it on the table next to the biscuit tin. "All we have to do is lightly color the page with a pencil."

"Do it!" ordered Tanya.

I dug out a pencil from the back of one of the kitchen drawers and rubbed the lead lightly over the empty top page.

"There's numbers coming through," Tanya whispered, nose almost touching the pad as she leaned across the table.

"Seven…no…eight numbers," said Ben, equally hypnotized.

"It's a clue," I said, disbelief in my voice as I stared down at the numbers. "We've got a real, fair-dinkum clue. Looks like a phone number."

"Well, don't just stand there," grumbled Ben, rubbing his hands together. "Ring the number. Find out who it belongs to."

Oh yeah. Easy peasy. Just ring the number.

"What if it's the killer?" Even to my own ears, my voice sounded as if I'd swallowed sand. This wasn't like reading about a murderer. This was real. Too damn real. "What if I recognize the killer's voice? That would mean I know him. Personally." I paused, heart-beat scooting up a couple of thousand decibels. "And worst scenario. What if the killer answered and he recognized *my* voice? What if—what if he knows I know he's the killer?"

By now I'd worked myself into such a state tiny beads of sweat littered my brow when I looked at my reflection in the toaster. I wiped my forehead with the back of my hand and stared down at the small sheet of yellow paper.

"Oh, gimme that!" Ben snatched the post-it note from the table and marched into the lounge room with Tanya and me trailing behind like toddlers on leads. "I'll ring the number myself."

With that, he lifted the receiver from its base and punched in the numbers—then waited.

Anxious to read any and all of the expressions on Ben's face when whoever was on the other end of the line answered, I perched on the arm of the sofa and leaned forward. The only outward signs of nervousness from Ben seemed to be the frown etched between his eyes, a twitch or two of his shoulders and the drum of impatient fingers on the wooden phone table.

"Hello. Who am I speaking to? Oooh…riiiight." A wide grin almost split Ben's face in two. "It's Cockatoo Pizza Palace on the line," he said and handed to phone to me. "So, unless they deliver their pizzas with large blunt instruments inside—I don't think we've found our killer yet."

I put the phone to my ear. "Can I take your order, please?" The girl on the other end of the line sounded bored and mechanical.

A great whooshing sigh of relief lurched through my body, leaving me limper than a bad handshake. "Er…yes… I'll have a family sized vegetarian please."

Tanya's mouth gaped as I finished placing the order and hung up. "Why did you order a pizza?"

"It's a pizza joint. What else was I supposed to do? Order a bucket of Macadamia ice cream and six bottles of Tequila?"

"No," put in Ben. "But you could have told them you'd dialed the wrong number." And then the image of a pizza with mozzarella cheese, capsicum, mushroom, onion, fresh and sun-dried tomato, fresh garlic and oregano topped off with special tomato sauce must have slid into his memory-bank. He smacked his lips. "Although, on second thoughts—"

"Yeah, on second thoughts," I agreed, smirking. "Vegetarian Pizza. Your absolute favorite. Now, let me put this another way. Are you hungry or do I have to eat this pizza all by myself?"

"Hungry?" returned Ben, drool forming on the corners of his lips. "Hell, I'm hungry enough to eat a swagman's bum through a wire fence."

"That's gross." I tried to visualize pink and white roses in a vase so Ben's image wouldn't compute. Beside me, the phone rang. Thinking it was Cockatoo Pizzas verifying my order, I picked up.

"Kat, this is Scott Brady, Liz's friend. I spoke to you a couple of days ago."

"Scott?" I frowned. "Don't you hippy types ever look at a clock? Do you realize it's half past two in the—"

"I know and I'm sorry. But please, don't fob me off this time. I'm really worried about Liz."

I sighed. Sank into the arm chair beside the phone and tried to ease the tension from my shoulders. "Go on then." My eyes strayed to my wrist where Liz's ruby bracelet told me something was very definitely wrong and it was up to me to do something about it. "Okay, I'm listening. What can you tell me?"

I could hear Scott take a deep breath before continuing. "That's the problem. I dunno what's happened to Liz. A couple of days ago, she phoned me. Said she was frightened. Something about overhearing a conversation she wasn't supposed to. Dunno what she was on about because she was babbling and before I could calm her down and find out what was up her nose, the phone went dead. I thought the battery in her mobile had crapped itself but when I drove out to check on her the next day, like, she was gone. Her stuff's still there but there's no sign of Liz."

Now nervous, my fingers played with the bracelet, twisted it back and forth. The tiny rubies set in the gold band glittered in the light from a floral lamp on the end-table beside me. "What makes you think Liz hasn't just taken off? You should know by now that my sister doesn't do conflict very well. Her normal reaction to any problem is to run away from it."

"The shack's been ransacked and I found blood on the floor."

I closed my eyes while a lump of lead settled in the pit of my stomach. "What are you trying to say, Scott?"

"What if Liz has been kidnapped or…"

The lump of lead grew heavier. "Or what?"

"I should have checked on her straight away instead of the next day."

"Have you contacted the police?"

"The local pigs aren't taking the case seriously. They think Liz, being a hippy, has moved on."

"They could be right."

"What about the blood? What about the mess in the shack?'

I forced myself to remain calm. "Scott, there's probably a simple explanation for the blood, like a nose bleed or maybe Liz cut herself. And as for the shack being ransacked—if you've lived with Liz for any length of time you should *know* she was born without a single housekeeping gene in her body."

There was a loud banging on the other end of the line. Sounded like someone hammering on Scott's front door. I strained to hear his words over the noise. "Kat, I found your phone number programmed into Liz's mobile—"

"You're kidding me. Liz has entered the twenty-first century?" *About time!* "And what—she left her mobile behind?"

"She left *everything* behind." Scott's voice gave a squeak of impatience then became serious again. "Look, strange things are happening here. Can't explain them over the phone but I think they're connected to the local greyhound track. I need you to help me find Liz." The banging became even louder and I could hear shouting. "Uh! Oh! Sorry, gotta go."

"Hang on!" I growled. "Where are you ringing from? Where in Port Augusta are you?"

His voice was barely a whisper. "Ring you later."

"Nooo!" I yelled. "I haven't heard from my little sister in over a year and you ring to tell me she's disappeared and then want to hang up on me. Do that, buster, and I'll put a deadly curse on you. You'll have warts growing out of your eyeballs and your toes will grow fungus and drop off."

Evidently he wasn't afraid of curses because all I could hear was the dial tone.

11

"Geez, Jake, shift up a gear, will ya?" I yelled, frustrated at the slow meanderings of my plodding dreadlocked assistant. "You run like a flippin' girl!"

It was the following morning, the sun was hanging low in the sky, and Jake and I were hand-slipping greyhounds—a training exercise that seemed to sustain my dogs' fitness for the race track. After barely three hours sleep, I was tired and irritable. Make that tired, irritable and jumpy. Maybe I could remove a couple of padlocks from Lofty's kennel and relax my vigilance on the two GAP dogs, even return Stella to her kennel by the gate and allow Stanley to join her after I'd picked him up from the vet—and maybe not.

Also, I couldn't get Liz's disappearance out of my mind.

Unanswered questions from the previous night buzzed in my brain. What was my sister's bracelet doing in Jack Lantana's house? If she'd simply moved on to greener pastures, why not take her backpack with her? Nausea swirled in the pit of my stomach as I acknowledged there might be something more sinister about Liz's disappearance than mere itchy feet.

Of course this meant I had to drive to Port Augusta and investigate. Not that there was any guarantee Liz was still there, but it was the last place she'd been seen. Scott implied something shady was going on at the greyhound track, so that's where I'd start nosing around and asking questions. Plus, even though Liz didn't think I was important enough to let me know we were now living in the same state, I guess it was up to me to set a bonfire under the Port Augusta police. So far, they didn't seem like they were too fussed by her disappearance.

And as for ringing Ma to discuss Liz's disappearance—I decided to put that unpleasant task off until I had more information.

Zorro, the dog clamped between my legs, let out a sharp bark and bounded forward, almost unseating me. I shook my head, tried to concentrate on straddling one bucking greyhound while attempting to calm the three barking, leaping, eager-to-get-going canines hooked to the chain wire fence beside me.

All eyes were on the runner. Jake.

I grit my teeth to stop from swearing. The manner in which my easy-going, dreadlocked, dude assistant was sauntering up the straight track which ran along the boundary of my property, I expected a snail to slither past him at any moment. And when he stopped and bent to pick something up from the ground—probably a half-squashed bug he thought needed saving—I let out a sigh. The dogs tied to the fence all wanted to gallop but I couldn't let them off until Jake reached the other end of my 300 meter slipping track. And at the rate he was traveling— we'd still be slipping dogs come dinner time.

Finally, Jake turned and even from a distance of a hundred yards I could see his crazy extra-wide grin. "Hey, man!" he shouted and held his 'find' in the air, waving it like a prized Olympic medal. "I just found a four leafed clover with, like, one leaf torn off!"

"Good for you," I yelled back clamping my knees more firmly around the torso of Zorro, the over-excited black youngster I struggled to hold. "Now, if you can tear yourself away from all that greenery, can you *please* get back to work? Otherwise, it'll be night time before we finish."

"Man, it's my lucky day." Jake tucked his four-leaf clover—minus one leaf—in the pocket of his T-shirt which proclaimed, 'Zero Tolerance to Chemicals in Food', and with leather dog leads flapping around his neck and shoulders, sprinted to the top of the track.

"Okay, Zorro, off you go." I unfastened the dog's collar and threw the lead on the ground behind me to free both hands. The black dog powered up the straight, every muscle straining and stretching to its limit. Boy could that youngster gallop. Couldn't wait for him to start racing. When Jake caught Zorro and tied him to the fence I unhooked dog number two, Molly—a racing dog coming back from a spell—and repeated the process.

Suzie, Zorro's hyperactive, white and black litter sister, screamed like she'd been ripped in half by a shark. My mobile rang. I let it go to message bank because Suzie had jumped so high in the air she'd come down with the lead wrapped around one leg. I unhooked her from the fence, told her she was as nutty as a Snickers bar, then let her go and grinned as she yipped and yapped the entire way up the straight. Suzie always reminded me of a dizzy blonde on speed.

Noting Suzie's safe arrival at the other end of the track, I left Jake to cool the dogs down and return them to their kennels. If I didn't collect Stanley from the vet soon, Dr. Terry Chapman, although a champion of GAP greyhounds, would be billing me for the dog's board and lodgings.

An hour later, I pulled up outside the local veterinary clinic and drove into the car park. Due to Purple Pants' demise my dogs were now relatively safe and Stanley, his little neutering operation completed, was all set to go to a loving adoptive home. Smiling, I pushed through the waiting room door and greeted Val, the receptionist, as she scurried in from the back entrance, long blonde hair a curtain across her face.

"What's up?" I asked and shook my head in mock horror. "Don't tell me that boss of yours got his arm stuck up another cow's rear end and you had the fun job of pulling it out?"

Val rolled her eyes toward the ceiling. "That was last week's party trick." She squatted to store clean towels in a bottom cupboard then straightened, shoved her hair from her eyes with one hand and stretched the kinks from her back. "Is it time to go home yet?"

I laughed. Val, the vet's normally cool, not a hair out of place receptionist, was really in a tizzy.

She let out an exasperated breath. "It's been one of those mornings," she confided through gritted teeth. "You know, vacuum cleaner on the blink, pushy salesman running off at the mouth until I wanted to shove a packet of dog biscuits down his throat to shut him up, two emergencies, plus a pile of dirty towels and an uncooperative washing machine." She took a deep replenishing breath and dragged the appointment book across the counter toward her. "Umm…let's see. At the moment Terry's with an obese French poodle. Shouldn't be long."

"No need to bother him, Val. I'm only here to pick up Stanley, one of the GAP dogs."

"Sorry, direct orders. Boss said to make sure I let him know as soon as you came in. He tried to ring you a couple of times this morning but you didn't pick up."

I thought of the calls I'd let go to message bank and hadn't got around to checking. My cheerful smile melted like chocolate in the sun as I contemplated the fact that greyhounds were extremely vulnerable to anesthetic. Oh God, no. Something must have gone wrong with Stanley's operation.

"It's Stanley, isn't it?" My voice caught in my throat as I leaned across the counter, inches from grabbing the front of Val's sky blue button up uniform and demanding more information. "What happened to Stanley?"

"Jesus, Kat, no need to have a coronary. Last time I checked on Stanley he was bored witless but otherwise fine. Tried seducing me with one of his hopeful, *I'm starving* faces but when I refused to go buy him a chocolate ice cream cone he went back to chewing on the wire. That dog is definitely good-to-go."

My heart, flopping like a hooked fish, went back to merely twitching before settling reluctantly back in its place. Much more stress and the poor thing would be off looking for another chest cavity to call home. I shook my head. "Well, if Stanley's okay…what's the problem?"

"Not sure." Val shrugged one shoulder as she brought up an account on her computer. "Terry discovered something while examining Stanley prior to his op. But don't worry, he'll explain everything to you as soon as he finishes his consultation with Mrs. Cruskit and her chocoholic French poodle."

"Explain what?" Dr. Terry Chapman, preceded by a fluffy, big haired woman that proved the theory people *do* look like their dogs, exited the nearest door and tossed a big bone-melting smile in my direction. "Ah there you are, Kat," he bellowed. "Just the person I wanted to see."

"Why? What's happened?"

Before I could start pumping Terry for information he turned to his departing client, her overwhelming cloud of Passion perfume causing both Val and me to surreptitiously hold our breath. Face grave, he shook one finger at the woman. "Now, remember what I told you, Mrs. Cruskit. *Lady Lala* and chocolate frogs do not agree. The ingredients in chocolate can be very dangerous for dogs."

"Oh, my poor, poor baby," Mrs. Cruskit simpered. "The big bad doctor said I can't give you any more chokky. Come on, darling, Mummy will carry you to the car." Bending, she picked up her wheezing poodle and made for the door, scraps of dog spilling from her soft fleshy arms.

The vet shook his head at the woman's departing back. "I mean it, Mrs. Cruskit—if you don't put Lala on the diet I recommended and walk her twice a day, you could lose her."

With one hand holding the door open, he beckoned me into his surgery.

"You okay?" he asked, concern crinkling his forehead as I brushed past him and entered the room.

"Never felt better."

"Liar, liar, pants on fire." One eyebrow hitched skyward, he peered down his nose at me. "Come on, Kat, I know about you and Tanya finding that man's body in a refrigerator. It's all over Facebook."

I closed my eyes. This couldn't be happening. So much for keeping my recent crappy life a secret. Oh for the good old days—the days before social networking made everyone's life an open book. "Did you also hear that we spent time in a holding cell rubbing shoulders with prostitutes, men in drag, and drug pushers?"

Terry shook his head. "No, but what I don't understand is what you and Tanya were doing inside the dead man's house at all?"

"I told you yesterday I was going to question the guy about why he was after my dogs." I paused but when Terry's lips pursed and his eyes narrowed, I quickly went on. "And when we got there his demonic guard dogs chased us into the house. It was a total nightmare."

"Which is why you need to be more careful." Terry sighed, indicated a chair for me and perched his butt on the desk. "Now, I don't know if this has anything to do with the case, but did you know Stanley's ear brands have been tampered with?"

"No." I shook my head. "Can't say I bothered to look."

"Before I began the operation, I checked the dog's ear brands and noticed the last number in his left ear had been changed."

"Why would anyone do that?"

"Well… I have a theory. Maybe—"

"Sorry to interrupt, Terry, but an emergency has just come in." It was Val, popping her head around the doorway. "Mrs. Davies cat got squashed when it bumped into a farm vehicle and several bags of wheat fell on top of it. The cat was chasing a bird, ripped off the bird's legs and Mrs. Davies has brought both the squashed cat and the legless bird in." She screwed up her nose. "Neither patient looks good."

Terry scrambled to his feet and preceded me to the door. "Bring them straight in, Mrs. Davies and I'll see if I can save them." He turned to Val. "I'll need your help with this—but first, can you please get Stanley for Kat?"

"No, no, don't bother." I insisted. "You need Val here. I can get Stanley."

"Okay, you'll find him in the last cage on the left." Terry stopped, placed one hand on my arm and gave a reassuring squeeze. "You know, I honestly think now Jack Lantana's out of the picture, Stanley will be safe."

"Let's hope so."

"But whatever happens, young lady, I want you to promise you'll be careful."

"I'll try."

Leaving Terry to care for the two emergency patients, I fossicked in my tote for Stanley's collar and lead then strolled across to the door on the other side of the waiting room.

The door was painted a flat white with the words Animal Hospital etched in black letters across the top. I'd been visiting the clinic the morning Val chose the two cartoon stickers pasted each side of the lettering—a cute but scruffy Thelwell dog and a twinkly-eyed Cat in the Hat.

Stanley would be so pleased to see me.

Smiling, I turned the brass handle and entered the large cool room. Immediately a lemony disinfectant smell snipped at my nose and the piercing yap of a pocket-sized Chihuahua assailed my ears. Cages, deep in shredded paper lined the four walls. A fluffy black and white rabbit with a twitching nose and one leg in plaster regarded me with curious black eyes from the first cage. On the indigo colored wall straight ahead squatted a large painting of a scene from Gawler's main street in the 1900s—men wearing dark three piece suits and hats—women in long, God-knows-how-they-kept-them-clean dresses—and horse-drawn carriages parading sedately along the dirt road.

Time to rescue my ever-hungry GAP dog; buy him a double decker ice cream and maybe a cheese-burger before taking him home to the 'welcoming committee'.

"Okay, Stanley," I joked. "I'm here to bust you outta the pen."

My eyes cut to the cages on the left—past two mewing cats and a snoring Yorky terrier to the last cage in the row.

The cage with the door hanging open…

And no Stanley inside.

12

I BLINKED. WIDENED MY EYES. Scanned every shadow in the recovery room. And even though the scan came up empty, my brain stubbornly blocked the logic—refusing to make sense of the information my eyes were processing.

Surely, Stanley must be hiding. Or someone was playing a cruel joke. But one more scrutiny of the empty cage and the empty room and I knew this nightmare wasn't over.

At that moment, Val pushed through the door of the animal hospital, a small brown bottle of pills in her hand. "Nearly forgot. These are Stanley's antibiotics. One tablet morning and—" She stopped, frowned, obviously perturbed by the wide-eyed panicked expression on my face.

"Stanley's gone," I told her, my voice barely above a whisper.

Open mouthed, Val stared at the empty cage and then let out a yell that reverberated through the room. "Terry! Come quick! Kat's dog isn't in here! He's gone!"

"Gone? Gone where?" Disbelief made Terry's voice harsh as he bullocked his way through the cartoon-labeled door into the sterility of the animal hospital.

"I don't know," said Val, her voice small and worried. "He was in his cage when I checked half an hour ago. And…and now his crate's empty and he's nowhere in the room." She twisted her hands together and her gaze, pleading forgiveness, swung across to me. "I'm so sorry, Kat. Whoever took him must have come in while I was out back washing the towels."

Tears welled behind my eyes and I covered my face with both hands. What if the dog-napper was Jack's murderer? If so, he was a hundred times more dangerous than the geriatric guy in purple pants. In fact, after what I'd seen in that refrigerator—my sweet lovable GAP dog's life would mean less than unwanted gum on the killer's shoes.

Hand shaking, I dug into my back pocket, feeling for my mobile. Time to bring in the Big Guns.

Time to contact DI Adams.

*****

The Colombo look-alike slouched against the wall of my dog kennels, frowning at the four heaped bowls of meat and kibble balanced in my arms. Spiral notebook in hand, he scratched behind his left ear before digging into his multiple coat pockets, doubtless in search of a writing instrument.

"Right," he said producing a squashed cigarette butt, sniffing its stale fragrance then stashing his find into an inside coat pocket. "Now, tell me exactly what happened at the vet's today."

I shook my head. *Now* he wanted to know. After Stanley's disappearance, I'd speed dialed Detective Inspector Adams to report the dog's disappearance. Huh. May as well have sent my message via a tottering old aged pensioner equipped with a generic-issue walking frame with two wonky wheels. I narrowed my eyes at the detective. Had Adams rushed to the vet surgery with lights flashing and sirens blaring? Nope. Had the slouching detective taken finger prints at the crime scene? Nope again. Had he organized patrols equipped with machine guns to hunt down the dog-napper? Ya gotta be kidding! Instead, when I rang he'd let out a string of unprintable curse words and told me to get the hell off the line because he was in the middle of a drug bust. Then, just before hanging up he said—*if* he had time—he'd be around to see me later in the day.

I glanced at the battery operated clock on the nearest wall. The clock with hands shaped like racing greyhounds in full flight. I'd discovered this kitschy piece in one of several dusty boxes at the local Op shop and it made me smile so I'd bought it for my temporary kennel house.

Almost 5 pm—definitely later in the day. Six hours since Stanley had disappeared from the recovery room at Terry Blackburn's veterinary surgery. My narrow eyed look turned into a scowl. Hell, by this time, the dog-napper could have caught a plane to the north of Australia and be rounding up kangaroos to slaughter for fun along the Dingo-proof and may never be found.

I was in the middle of feeding my racing team and couldn't stop to talk to Adams and his surly female companion, Constable Belinda Chalmers. Didn't fancy the roof of the kennel house lifting off and landing up the road, due to disgruntled barking. So I answered their questions while I worked.

I juggled the dishes in my arms, then straightened to my full height of five feet five, which was still a good six inches shorter than DI Adams. "I told you what happened, Inspector. Someone stole my dog."

Adams produced a basic blue ballpoint pen from a deep pocket in his long overcoat and flipped a new page open in his spiral notebook. "Could your missing dog have pushed the door of his cage open and escaped?"

"No, I told you over the phone, Stanley was dog-napped." I opened the nearest kennel door, slid a bowl of beef, kibble and vitamins inside—to the excitement of a bouncing, barking Zorro—refastened the kennel door, repeated the procedure three more times and then turned to Detective Adams, hands on hips. "Even if Stanley managed to rattle his cage door loose, there's no way he could have escaped from the recovery room. The dog may be bright but even *he* doesn't know how to turn the knob on a door."

"Hmm…"

I sent him an accusatory scowl. "If you remember, I told you at the police station last night my dogs were under threat. You took no notice. And now look what's happened… Stanley has been kidnapped."

"Hmm…" he said again as he scratched on the paper with his ballpoint pen, discovered it had no ink, and began to delve into his coat pockets for another. "Maybe that was because I was more interested in the fact that you and your over-indulging friend had discovered the body of a murder victim." He hitched one eyebrow. "Inside a house you'd broken into."

I shook my head in frustration, barely refraining from stamping my foot like a tetchy two-year-old. "Tanya and I did *not* break in—we were chased into the house by Lantana's guard dogs. I told you that too." I turned away from him to snaffle four more food bowls from the table beside the fridge. "Don't you *ever* listen?"

While I fed the last of the yapping dogs, the Inspector's questions continued. Not that he listened to any of my answers. It was like having a discussion with a stone statue. Finally, I decided to reverse the role and ask some questions myself.

"As you have no intention of adding Stanley to your *Missing* list, let's talk about the missing human. My sister, Liz. Have you heard anything from the Port Augusta police about her disappearance?"

DI Adams scratched at his stubbly five o'clock shadow. "Actually…"

"*We're* asking the questions, Ms. McKinley," snapped Constable Chalmers who'd been unusually quiet up until now. Perhaps she wasn't keen on the unblinking stare the black and white greyhound in the end kennel was giving her. Note to self: if Chalmers gives me any trouble let Rastus out of his kennel, then sit back and enjoy the show. Chalmers had special pheromones that seemed to attract all male dogs. And Rastus was no exception.

"The Port Augusta police are exploring all possibilities but haven't come up with a strong lead yet," DI Adams admitted. "This isn't the first time your sister has disappeared you know. That Scott fellow reported her missing once before and she was found hugging a tree scheduled to be cut down, twenty miles away."

"Oh." Could Liz be doing something similar now? Out hugging trees or chaining herself to an old soon-to-be-demolished building? But that still didn't answer the question of why her bracelet was in Jack Lantana's house. Or could Ben be right? Was it a coincidence and Lantana had merely found Liz's bracelet on the street where she'd dropped it?

Adams broke into my thoughts. "And that Scott fellow isn't what he seems either."

"What do you mean?"

"Scott Brady has a record. The man might only be in his early twenties but he's already spent a couple of stints in jail. Burglary, and assault with a weapon." DI Adams shook his head. "If I were you I wouldn't be inviting your sister's boyfriend home for a Sunday roast."

"I don't *do* Sunday roasts." I ran the hot water in the sink and added a large squirt of Liquid-Fresh, ready to wash the dogs' dishes—even though most had been licked so clean they sparkled.

DI Adams shuffled his feet before raising both eyebrows. "And I'd be warning that sister of yours to watch out for him."

"Gotta find her first," I reminded him and stood, hands on hips, as I watched him bury his notebook in a deep pocket inside his overlarge overcoat. "So…you're not going to do anything about finding my dog, are you?"

"It's on my 'to-do' list," he said then his gaze hardened and his frown deepened. "But it's *not* on yours." He took two steps closer, leaning right into my face. I could smell the lingering tanginess of his aftershave and spotted a small nick on his chin where he'd miscued while shaving. "Which means, I do *not* want to find you asking questions or getting involved in this case in any way. Do I make myself clear?"

"But it's *my* sister and *my* dog that's—"

"Ms. McKinley… Kat…there's a very inventive, cold blooded killer out there. A killer who wouldn't think twice about chopping you into very small pieces, packing the blood soaked chunks into a plastic container and mailing them off to your mother." He hitched one eyebrow, never dropping eye contact. "Am I scaring you?"

Scaring me? Hell, he had me almost wetting my pants.

I nodded.

"Good."

I gave him a weak smile, attempting to bring some humor into the present horror-show. "Chopping Guy would need to affix the right amount of stamps on the parcel, otherwise—knowing what a cheapskate my mother is—she'd refuse to pay excess postage." My smile held on like Tarzan's Grip. "What do you think, DI Adams? Would the post office send the package back—or bury me in the Dead Letter Office?"

My favorite Colombo-look-alike detective didn't bother answering. Instead, he just hunched his shoulders, then indicating with a head flick to his assistant that the interview was over, stomped out.

13

DI Adam's cautionary words reverberated in my head—creeped me right out—so much so, as I loosed each dog into emptying yards before bedding them down for the night, my overactive imagination upped the terror and turned it into a horror movie. A Freddy Kruger movie on steroids—with me, the latest vulnerable victim, cowering on center stage, while the villain, his sharp silver axe dripping blood, crouched in every cupboard, lurked in every shadow, hid behind every tree.

His goal—to hack chunks from the body I loved—mine—and methodically pack the severed pieces in a parcel addressed to Mother.

After locking up, I grabbed a short sharp breath and trudged along the dirt path toward the house. Hunched inside myself. Fighting the urge to break into a mad ungainly sprint and bolt for the front door. Why had I planted so many trees and bushes on either side of this path? They created too many shadows. Too many gnarled twisted boughs that resembled a man's arms reaching out for me. First thing in the morning, I'd pay Mr. Turner from next door to drive his tractor over and bulldoze the lot.

Was Adams right? Should I endanger my life to investigate Liz's disappearance only to find she'd chained herself to some threatened hundred and fifty-year-old gum, marked with an x, due to tree rot? Liz probably wouldn't even leave the damn tree to attend my funeral.

But she *was* my sister. And she *was* missing.

And so was Stanley.

Were Liz, Stanley and Jack's killer all connected? My brain did a quick lap of the mental trail, banged into several insurmountable hurdles, burnt and crashed—still with no answers.

Surreptitiously checking over both shoulders for a shadowy boogey man sneaking up on me with a raised axe, I ducked inside the house, locked and secured the front door with a security chain and turned on several lights. But I still didn't feel safe. Not until my two house-pets, plus Stella, had been let into the house and I'd turned the key in the back door.

Whew! After toeing off my old sneakers and tossing my battered yard parka onto the back of a kitchen chair, I regarded the dogs bouncing around my feet, threatening to upend me due to their one-track-minds.

"Right, guys, I know—it's past your dinner time, but you're not likely to collapse of hunger," I told my tap dancing cheer squad while filling three doggy bowls with beef and kibble and then placing them on the colorful linoleum, several yards apart. "And Lucky," I warned the tail wagging black greyhound whose drool was currently threatening to flood the kitchen, "keep out of the other dogs' food— especially Tater's bowl—or you're likely to lose that cheeky black nose. You know that little guy's not a sharer."

Thank goodness there was no need to bring out the First Aid kit tonight. Within seconds Tater had licked his bowl clean and by the time Lucky slunk over to investigate his bowl, Tater was over helping Stella give her dish a final polish. I grinned. My lion-hearted Tater may be a teacup Chihuahua—but he'd always be King of the McKinley household.

Dogs fed, I rummaged in the freezer until I found a frozen turkey dinner to nuke in the microwave. The turkey dinner came complete with little roast potatoes, green peas and carrots and promised gourmet taste, no artificial colors or flavors and a full day's quota of calories, protein and carbohydrates. I closed my eyes to the fat and sodium levels. Hey, I'd likely work those off next time Ben and I adjourned to the bedroom.

Twenty minutes later, when the phone trilled its annoying interruption, I was slumped on the couch with my feet on an ottoman, enjoying my white meat and veggies and completely absorbed as the chained magician submerged himself in a tank of water on the Grand Final of *Australia's Got Talent*. Damn. Who could be ringing during my favorite show? So inconsiderate. Should be a law against it. I knew it wouldn't be Tanya. She'd be barricaded in the house—glued to her lounge chair—Erin at a friend's house—all phones switched off—and rooting for the sexy magician to win the final.

With my tray of food balanced on my lap—no way could I put it down with three oh-so-hungry canines eyeing my every mouthful—I picked up. If this was a cold caller wanting to sell me the Sydney Harbour Bridge, I'd slam the receiver down so hard their ears would be ringing for weeks.

"Yeah."

"Good evening, Kat, you left a message for me to ring."

Oh-uh! It was Gina Robertson, the coordinator of GAP. When Stanley went missing, I'd left Gina a message to ring me, but with the arrival of DI Adams, I'd forgotten to follow up with another call.

"I hope there's no problem with either of the two GAP dogs in your care?" Gina's voice was ultra-pleasant. Everything about Gina was ultra-pleasant and yet some days her smile didn't quite reach her eyes. I knew this was going to be one of those days.

"Um… Stella will be ready to go in a couple of days," I said hoping to prolong the discussion on Stanley. "She's amazing inside the house and as soon as her stitches are out she'll be ready to make someone a gorgeous pet."

"That's excellent news. I have a family with three children who can't wait to adopt Stella. I've inspected their premises and the dog will have a loving home with the best of care. One of the children showed me what they've already bought for their new pet. Two new rugs—one for home and one for going out—new food bowls, chew toys, squeakers, a giant bag of kibble, a freezer full of beef…you name it…the Taylors have already thought of it." Gina paused. "Now, what about Stanley?"

Yeah. *What about Stanley?*

"I'm sorry," I said and licked my dry lips. "We have a problem with Stanley."

There was a pause before Gina spoke and when she did her voice had changed from ultra-pleasant to what I'd call steely. And it sounded like she was forcing the words through gritted teeth. "A problem?"

"I'm afraid he's gone missing."

"Gone missing?"

If she was going to repeat everything I said this phone conversation would get old very quickly. "Gina," I took a deep breath and let my confession burst out. A water tank overflowing after a rain storm. "I should have let you know earlier, but I thought the dog-napper was after my top racing dog, Big Mistake—not the GAP dogs. You see, over the last couple of days this man, who I've never seen before, has been trying to steal Stanley. He even dog-napped Stella by mistake then brought her back. It was so scary I kept both dogs locked inside my house. Anyway, that man was murdered last night and today Stanley's gone missing. He was taken from Terry Blackburn's vet surgery and—"

I let the gabbling run down, took a deep breath and waited for the yelling. Nothing. The *nothing* went on for a full minute. My hands were sweaty and I could feel bad vibes slithering up through the phone lines. Gina evidently wasn't going to help me out here so I took the bull by the horns, as my Granny McKinley would say. "Gina, do you have any idea *why* or *who* would be interested in stealing Stanley?"

"Me? How would I know? I hope you're not insinuating that I'm involved with Stanley's disappearance?" There was definite steel in her voice now plus an itty bitty squeak.

"I'm not insinuating anything. Just asking if you know why Stanley is so important that someone stole him. And maybe even killed because of him."

"Katrina, calm down. I think you are being overly dramatic. Dogs go missing all the time." Gina's voice was ultra-pleasant once again but there was something about her acceptance of the situation that made me think maybe she knew something after all. "Stanley is probably running the streets raiding rubbish bins as we speak. Did you ring the RSPCA to see if they've picked him up?"

"No, because the dog did *not* let himself out. The door of the vet surgery was closed. There's no way even Stanley could turn that handle."

"Well, maybe the receptionist—what's her name, Val—accidently let Stanley out and is too afraid of losing her job to admit to it."

"That's ridiculous, and you know it. Val's too responsible and conscientious to let a patient on her watch escape and…and if she did…there's no way Val would put me through this agony. She'd confess. Job or no job."

"Alright, Katrina, this is not your concern. Leave it with me. I'll contact Animal Welfare in the morning and take it from there. It's not your fault. No need for us to fall out. After all, Stanley is only a dog. And we have plenty more GAP dogs to care for and place in new homes without letting this situation cloud our main goal."

With that she hung up.

I shook my head. Blinked down at the phone as though it was instrumental in fabricating that weird conversation. *Stanley? Only a dog?* That didn't sound like the Gina Robertson who worked countless hours on a voluntary basis to run the State's GAP program. The Gina Robertson whose tongue lashings could make even the biggest, strongest man quake if she caught him neglecting or being cruel to one of our precious greyhounds.

I slowly settled the receiver back on its base and eyed the television screen. Six lithe young men dressed in nothing from the waist up were twisting and gyrating their bodies in time to some disjointed rap-like music, but my mind barely registered the bare flesh and the tight six-packs. My mind couldn't get past Gina's uncharacteristic words.

A chill, deep and biting, infiltrated my chest and spread its tentacles into my limbs.

I shivered and reached for the fluffy dark blue blanket spread across the back of the sofa.

Gina Robertson knew something about Stanley's disappearance and it had her running scared. Maybe she also knew something about my sister's disappearance. Or how the geriatric guy ended up dead in his own refrigerator.

But what made me snuggle deeper under that fluffy blue blanket was the fact that I'd decided to visit GAP's ultra-pleasant coordinator first thing in the morning and try to find out what that something was.

14

IY WAS TEN O'CLOCK THE FOLLOWING MORNING. Although dark clouds scudded across the sky, threatening rain, it wasn't cold. Somewhere between 18 and 20 degrees. Compared to European countries, Australian winters were mild, with temperatures varying from zero to low twenties.

I changed out of my work clothes of ancient ripped jeans and tatty T into new straight-leg jeans, a pale apricot tunic top that Ben said highlighted my hazel-green eyes, and folded a light synthetic slicker into my tote bag, just in case the skies *did* open.

The racing dogs were worked and fed and I'd decided the best excuse for dropping in on Gina, uninvited, was to deliver Stella to her kennels. After all, with Stanley dognapped it was only wise I made sure Stella was safe over the next couple of days. Her new family would be devastated if anything happened to her.

I'd brushed the dog's red brindle coat until it shone and fastened a soft green leather, GAP collar around her neck. Stella knew she was going out. In fact she became so excited she rushed around the house, her over-active tail knocking into the furniture as she bounced and barked at Tater, who was trying to keep up with her much longer legs.

Of course I couldn't get out of the house with only one dog. The looks on Lucky and Tater's faces told me exactly what they thought of *that* idea.

Okay, we'd go as a family.

First, I put the back seat down in the Holden station wagon as it was too dangerous to have two loose greyhounds bouncing around, stomping on Tater and causing major arguments while I drove. Then I strapped Tater in the middle of the back seat with a greyhound on each side. All safely harnessed.

"Right guys?" I asked checking them out over my shoulder after turning the key in the ignition. "Everyone comfortable back there?"

Tater rolled his eyes and gave the doggy equivalent of a pout. His tiny sharp featured face registering disapproval at being jammed in between the lolling-tongued greyhounds in the back, instead of in his usual position beside me in the passenger's seat.

To keep any disagreements by 'the kids' to a minimum, I sang along with Good Charlotte on the car radio as we drove towards Williamstown. Occasionally Lucky tried to join in but her voice was strident and flat. Each time she started, Tater snapped at her as if to say, *Button up, Bucko.*

However, by the time I parked in the sloping driveway of Gina's rolling hundred acre property on the outskirts of Williamstown, my nerves had returned. Butterflies fluttered in my stomach battering against the walls, wanting out. How was I supposed to question Gina, ask her what she knew about Liz, Stanley, and the dead guy in the refrigerator? If my theory was wrong she'd think I was crazy—probably call the men in white and have me institutionalized.

And if I was right—why would she tell me anything—more likely hit me on the head and lock me up in one of her isolated sheds then flush the key down the loo.

I switched off the motor, told the excited canines in the back seat to wait while I scoped the place out and opened the door of the car. Immediately, three elderly greyhounds trotted arthritically over to greet me, smiles of welcome accompanied by wagging tails and slurps of affection. These were Gina's personal 'keepers'—dogs she'd adopted years ago when they first came out of racing. During the day the geriatric trio had freedom of the property and at night a warm soft bed inside the house. Of course I had to pat each individual gray head and insist they were the most beautiful animals in the whole world, before pushing through a couple of inquisitive pigs, Choco, a piebald miniature pony Gina had rescued from a suburban garage where he hadn't seen the light of day for two years, and her favorite rescue animal—Atticus the goat. What she saw in Atticus I'd never know. He was a nasty piece of work with a one-track mind. And that was lowering his head and butting bums.

There were raised voices coming from inside the barn where Gina kept several rescue horses all needing care and treatment before going to new homes. That was Gina. Anything from an injured kangaroo to a broken winged seagull found a home with her. Which is why her comment of, 'Stanley's only a dog', didn't ring true.

Was someone blackmailing her?

Threatening her?

Dodging Atticus's horns I hurried across to the barn and shook the door. Locked. Now that was unusual. Although the voices were raised, I could only hear one or two words through the thickness of the barn door. Not enough to know if I needed to ring for help. However, it was definitely Gina and a man with a gruff voice. And they were arguing.

But who was in there with her? Why was the door locked? Was Gina being held against her will?

A ladder stood against the side of the barn with a large tin of forest green paint balanced on the top rung. Unlike me, Gina was forever painting her outbuildings. Being a klutz, I left that messy task to Jake. It seemed as soon as Gina finished painting every shed on her property, it was time to start all over again—just like the Sydney Harbour Bridge. But the thing that drew me toward the ladder was the fact that there was a two inch gap between the top of the barn wall and the roof, left that way for air circulation. If I could climb the ladder, maybe I'd see who was in the barn with Gina. And whether I needed to call the cavalry or not.

Skirting around a buzzing pile of manure, as exotic smelling as a sewer in summer, I placed one foot on the bottom rung of the ladder and took a deep breath. Was I doing the right thing? Shouldn't I just bang on the barn door and call out?

But I wanted to see who was in the barn. Who was arguing with Gina. If I let them know I was outside, the man might hide, or worse still, hurt Gina. So I carefully put one foot in front of the other until I stood on the top rung of the ladder, beside the tin of green paint.

The voices were much clearer from this vantage point.

"For God's sake, Gina, get off my case. I don't know what the hell you're talking about."

"Don't bullshit me, Garry, you snake-in-the-grass. You promised no dogs would be hurt! Where is he? Where have you stashed him? If you don't bring him here to me I'll start talking." I could hear the anger bubbling in Gina's voice as I stretched an extra two inches to get a better view inside the shed.

Was this a man who'd shown cruelty to one of her many rescue dogs—or something more sinister? I placed one eye in the two inch space at the top of the building. Gina stood, hands on hips, face the color of burnt ashes, her body like a coiled spring. A tall skinny guy dressed in grungy oil-stained jeans and a leather jacket, his back to me, leaned into her space.

"Watch my lips, Gina, 'cos I'm only gunna say this the once. I can't protect you if you keep interfering. So…back the fuck off!"

Eyes fastened on the man's back, trying to memorize every line, every strand of his long greasy strawberry blonde pony-tailed hair, the too tight fit of his dirty jeans, the jagged rip on the right shoulder of his black leather jacket and the color of his raspberry red socks showing between scuffed brown shoes and the bottom of his frayed jeans, I reached into my back pocket for my mobile.

Which is when the ladder wobbled from side to side.

Oh! Uh! I glanced down at the ground, a scary eight feet below me and let out a yell. Silence suddenly unimportant as fear took over. "Nooo Atticus! Get away from the ladder!"

But of course Atticus had selective hearing. With a smirk that told me I was in deep trouble, the evil goat lowered his head and butted the ladder again.

And again.

Calling him every name in the Australian Book of Swearwords, I clung onto the wooden sides of the ladder and closed my eyes. Why me? Why now? Why did my efforts at sleuthing always land me in the shit?

And then I did. Land in the shit, that is. Or to be more precise—flat on my face in the middle of the stinking manure pile, coughing and spluttering as the smell and taste of rotting manure invaded every crevice of my face, forced itself up both nostrils and entered my open mouth as I screamed.

Aaaaaagh....

"Trying to fly, Katrina?"

Spitting and coughing, I looked up, wiped animal waste from both eyes and saw Gina, brows up around her hairline, dark eyes definitely not smiling. Heard a motor bike start up, splutter a couple of times then take off from around the back of the barn and screech past us out of the gateway. But I was too busy heaving my guts out, as the flavor and perfume of week-old shit caught in my throat, to answer Gina's question or note what color and make of bike the man with the red socks was riding.

Nose squinching in distaste, Gina helped me to my feet and pointed to a nearby hose attached to a faucet outside the barn. "Might want to clean up," she said. "I'll see if I can find you a towel."

Evidently not keen on having me anywhere near her house, Gina entered the barn and came out seconds later with a couple of freshly washed horse-towels and a clean chaff bag.

Seemed like a nice hot shower in her newly tiled bathroom was out of the question today.

"Why are you here?" she asked. "And what the hell were you doing up the ladder? And don't say painting, because you wouldn't know which end of a paint brush to use."

After squirting my face, arms and hands, I toweled myself dry and looked down at my ruined clothes. Never again would I be able to wear Ben's favorite apricot tunic top. And as for getting the foul smell of horse poop out of my hair—it would take a full bottle of Coconut shampoo and a week's worth of hot water.

Gina was still staring at me. Waiting for answers that I didn't have. But shouldn't I be the one asking the questions? One look at Gina's face said otherwise. "Umm… I brought Stella over," I said and waved toward my car. "I was passing this way so thought I'd save you the trouble of picking her up. And-and when I couldn't find you I climbed the ladder to see if you were inside the barn."

Geez, even to my ears that excuse sounded like a pathetic lie.

Gina's eyes never left mine. They bored into me and I could tell she knew I'd been eavesdropping and when she spoke her voice was edgy. "Okay, I'll get Stella out of the car and introduce her to the other GAP dogs," she said and passed me the chaff bag. "Here, take this. You'll need it to put on the seat of your car because if you sit on your upholstery you'll never get the stink out."

With that she took off and while I trudged behind her clutching the chaff bag in one hand and fending off Atticus with the other, she undid Stella's harness and let her jump out of the car.

Of course when Stella scampered off with the Geriatric Trio and the inquisitive pigs, Tater and Lucky set up a commotion. They wanted out too. So I quickly arranged the bag on the front seat, slid behind the wheel and turned the key in the ignition. Time to go home, hit the shower and attempt to work out how this newest piece of jigsaw fit into the overall puzzle.

I eased my foot onto the accelerator and leant out the window. "See you, Gina. Sorry I spilt your paint and made such a huge dent in your manure pile."

"Kat," she said and touched me on the shoulder, expression grim, voice clipped. "Forget what you heard today. Okay? If you play the Nancy Drew gambit you'll be sorry."

I blinked at Gina's words. Was that warning or threat? A shiver caused me to reach across and turn the car heater on full blast.

But I came here to get answers. If I drove off like a chicken with no head, afraid to tackle Gina, find out what she knew about Stanley's disappearance, I may as well take up macramé instead of sleuthing. I sighed and put the car back into Park.

"No, you can't get rid of me that easily, Gina. What's going on? Was that man threatening you? Did he steal Stanley?"

Gina shook her head. Took a step away from the car. "You think, because you solved the last mystery, you know what you're doing. Well, let me tell you—you haven't a clue. You almost got yourself killed last time and you're heading that way again. Just keep your nose out of it."

"I can't do that. A dog on my watch has disappeared and I think you know more than you're telling me about Stanley's disappearance."

"As I told you before—leave it to me." And then her voice softened. "I'd never forgive myself if they hurt you too."

With that she spun on her heel and trekked across the yard toward the kennels. The dogs, the inquisitive pigs, the pony, and Atticus the goat, trailing along behind her.

Gina Robertson—the Pied Piper of animals—but was she leading the animals to safety or destruction?

15

An hour and a half later, I'd scrubbed myself raw, changed into black trackie bottoms and a colorful blue, green and yellow sloppy pullover. Although still with a slight, unmistakable but impossible to eradicate, odor, I got back in the car and headed for the small country town of Virginia—a ten minute drive from Two Wells.

By now, the threatening rain clouds of the morning had burst their seams. As I parked outside *The Luv Bug*, sending water splashing onto the footpath, I squinted through the wet windscreen. Was Tanya busy selling sex toys? Nope. I could see my best friend walking to nowhere on the second-hand treadmill she'd installed for times when trade at the adult shop was slow. And her boss, Norm the Nervous, was nowhere to be seen.

Good. Now I could run my latest news past her without big ears straining to hear our whispered conversation.

"Raining cats and dogs out there," I said as I shook the water from my hair.

"As long as you don't let the little varmints inside," Tanya joked, puffing a little as she walked. "And what brings you to my humble place of employment when you could be enjoying the pungent smell of wet dog and mud?"

Ignoring her banter, I got straight to the point. "I need your advice."

Tanya's eyebrows lifted, but she didn't break step. Tanned legs pumping under her micro-mini-skirt.

"I'm confused," I said. "There's this person I've always respected and—and I think she might be involved in something illegal. It's doing my head in."

The noisy thrum of rain bucketing down outside contributed to my present dark mood. Gina Robertson—savior of animals—squeaky clean administrator of our state's greyhound adoption program—maybe a Mob Mamma? That image didn't compute. I sighed as I pictured Gina arguing with the man in the barn, remembered her parting words to me, 'I'd never forgive myself if they hurt you too'.

They who?

God, I was a lousy detective. Every time I attempted to unearth the answer to one question—not only did I *not* get an answer, but another question popped up. It was like driving in circles in a foreign country-complete with not knowing the language.

"Well, I can't help you if you won't fill in the blanks," Tanya said waving one hand in front of my eyes while holding onto the bar of her walker with the other. "Snap out of your daze and tell me the name of this pillar of society who might or might not be a crook."

"It's Gina Robertson." Unable to keep still, I paced up and down in front of the counter, distractedly checking out the equipment on display. "She knows more about Stanley's disappearance than she's letting on and I don't know why she won't confide in me. After all, we're both on the same side."

"Hmm…sure about that?"

"Of course I am."

"What if Goodie-Two-Shoes is in this right up to her coral colored lipstick?"

"Tanya, just because you and Gina don't see eye-to-eye ever since you nicked her boyfriend—"

"Hey—I did *not* steal Corey Palmer. The guy was tired of playing second fiddle to the woman's goats, pigs and homeless dogs, so he moved on. It's as simple as that." She switched off the treadmill, stepped off and wiped the sweat from her face with a pink hand towel displaying a fit naked man in the act of bending over. "And it wasn't my fault he moved on to me."

"But then *you* moved on from *him*," I added. My best friend could be such a man-eating slut at times. "Look at this from Gina's point of view. You pinched her boyfriend, refused to give him back for three days and then when she declared it was over between them, you dumped the guy."

"Katrina, have you ever had three days of sex with a whiner?"

"Er…can't say I have."

Tanya folded her hand towel over the front bar of the treadmill and blew air through her lips. "It was like going shopping with your mother-in-law. *Why were you so quick? Why were you so slow? Oh, I wanted to be on top. No, no, the kitchen table's too hard.* Don't know how the sainted Gina put up with the Big Girl's Blouse bellyaching for so long."

I picked up a packet of jokey giant sized condoms that would fit an elephant and frowned. "So, what happened?"

"On the third day I decided to douse his skinny little willy in a vase of week-old water, complete with a dozen prickly roses." Tanya shrugged one bare shoulder and hitched at her boob tube. It was warm in the air-conditioning but I hoped she had a track-suit, coat and galoshes waiting in the closet for when she closed up shop. "And then I dumped him."

When God created Tanya—he broke the mold. Probably yanked on his Heavenly hob-nailed boots and kicked the stuffing out of it.

I gazed through the shop window. Two girls on horseback jogged along the wet roadway, bodies hunched under bright orange wet gear. A squally wind sent a soggy chip packet laboring across a puddle…

And when Ben, dark hair covered by a dripping Akubra hat, tugged open the shop door, a life-sized cardboard Marilyn Monroe look-alike taking pride of place in the middle of the store, crashed to the ground.

"Ladies," he drawled and removed his Drizabone before standing Marilyn back on her feet and giving her cardboard bottom a smack.

I couldn't stop the grin from spreading across my face. "Do that to all the girls?" I purred. "Or just the ones who can't smack you back?"

His dark eyes narrowed, implying I'd learn the answer to that question later.

"Aha, look what the wind blew in." Tanya smirked and marched behind the counter, her mock saleslady persona in place. "Double pronged vibrator?" she cooed. "Blow up doll? Girlie magazine? Name your weapon of choice, sir, and I'll see what I can dig up. Although, if you're after sex toys, Benjamin, I'm disappointed in you. Must mean you and Kat aren't getting your gear off enough at home."

Tanya discussed sex like most people discussed the weather. I ignored her. Not so, Ben. He winked, his expression clearly stating: *if we got our gear off any more, Miss Sexaholic, we'd both need walking frames to get around.* "No need for any of your equipment, Tan—I'm here to talk to Kat." He lifted an eyebrow at me and I swear he was *taking my gear off* mentally. "Jake told me you were at *The Luv Bug*," he said. "Also mentioned something about you being covered in shit."

"No comment. And remind me to dock Jake's pay. Anyway, what's up?"

Before Tanya could initiate a ribald play on words, Ben stepped into my space and placed both hands on my shoulders. Immediately the smell of wet tangy earth and spearmint gum invaded my nostrils. "You're determined to go to Port Augusta, aren't you?"

"And a good afternoon to you, too."

His dark eyes raked mine. "Don't deny it. I'm surprised you haven't already staked your tent out in the middle of the Port Augusta greyhound track ready to question the locals about Liz's disappearance."

"I can't just up and leave the dogs. And anyway, DI Adams says Liz hasn't disappeared at all. He thinks she's chained herself to a tree, protesting about developers denuding the forests. She's evidently done it before. He also advised me to leave finding her to the police."

"And of course you're heeding the cop's warning?"

Ben's fingers massaged my shoulders. Oooh…lovely…didn't realize my muscles were so tense. "Can you dig in a little deeper near the neck?"

"Adams hasn't a clue," Ben continued as he kneaded the muscles around my neck. "There again, he doesn't know you like I do. If he did, he'd lock you up for your own protection. Hell, *I'd* lock you up, but I know if I did, you'd hurt me—in ways that make me flinch even thinking about them—so—I've come up with plan A instead."

"Woohoo. Lock her up, Ben, go on. Don't be a spoil sport. I want to have a front seat view when she does the hurting."

"Plan A?" I queried, once again ignoring Tanya's sex obsessive comments.

"Five of my dogs are racing at the Port Augusta tomorrow. Come with me, help me handle the dogs, and I'll help you ask questions at the track about Liz, plus I'll be there to cover your back. What do you think?"

Warmth crept through me like a comforting hug. And it wasn't caused by the bone-melting shoulder rub that was presently making me purr. This guy was one of a kind. Unlike other men I'd had relationships with—Ben really got me.

"Thanks," I said and stood on tiptoe to kiss him. "I owe you."

Of course the kiss turned into a full on snog, with tongue, and would have developed further if we weren't standing in an adult sex shop in the middle of a small country town where anyone passing by would immediately hurry to the local supermarket and set the gossip mill rolling.

"Aargh. Will you two stop with the lovey-dovey stuff? It's sickening. Ya gunna make me toss me sport's drink in a minute." Tanya sounded exactly like Erin, her eleven-year-old daughter. "Kat, tell Ben how you ended up covered in horse poop."

"Hmm," Ben's grin crinkled the corners of his eyes. "This I have to hear. Okay, McKinley—give."

Damn. "Do I have to?"

Falling head first into a manure pile never looked good on one's life-resume. My kids would probably be laughing as they told the story to *their* kids in years to come. Of course, for that to happen, first I'd have to get over my paralyzing phobia of actually pushing an eight pound human from a cavity too small to accommodate a packet of gum.

I let out another sigh then reluctantly filled Ben in on the Perils of Katrina. When I reached the part where Atticus the goat caused my demise, I thought Ben would die laughing. In fact I had to chase him around the shop with a leather plaited BDSM whip to save his life.

"So, you reckon Gina is a suspect?" Ben said once he'd regained his breath and his dignity and impounded the whip.

"I don't know what to think. I agree, she's acting suspiciously, but I also know Gina would never hurt an animal."

"Come on, face it, Kat. Saint Gina is either a criminal—or she's stuck in the middle protecting someone who is." Tanya let out a laugh. "Oh no, don't tell me Miss Prim and Proper has found herself a bad boy lover and he's leading her astray."

"What do you reckon, Kat?" said Ben. "Did they seem intimate at all?"

Before I could think any more about the woman who ran the GAP program and her bizarre behavior with the stranger in the barn, my phone beeped, indicating I'd received a text. "Maybe," I concurred as I slid my mobile from my pocket, clicked on the phone and brought up the message.

L in trouble. Meet me at Pt Augusta track during race 6. I'll be in car park beside red VW Beetle. Come alone. Scott.

A chill prickled my spine.

How did Liz's boyfriend know I'd be at the track? More to the point—how did he know my mobile number—I'd recently changed the sim card so he couldn't have found it in Liz's little black book.

I tightened my grip on the phone. Was Liz really in trouble? Or was this a trick to get me in that car park. Alone. And—and do what?

The chill spread from my spine into the deep cavities of my chest. I drew in a deep breath, let it out slowly. Now, what did DI Adams tell me about Scott Brady? Something to do with serving time in jail for burglary and assault…

Swallowing the lump in my throat, I tapped Scott's number into my keypad. I'd sort this guy out once and for all—give him the third degree, chew him up, then spit out the pips. Ready to dredge up my inner Cybil, I jammed the phone to my ear.

But there was only dead air at the other end of the line.

16

AT FIVE THE NEXT MORNING, I stood at the kitchen table, breakfasting on a slice of toast and a giant mug of white coffee with four sugars. Cold hands wrapped around the warmth of my Simpsons' mug, I debated whether to confide in Ben about my coming meeting with Scott Brady. And decided against it. Unwise, perhaps, but being all macho man, Ben would insist on accompanying me to the car park and if Scott saw Ben, maybe he wouldn't show.

Bottom line—I needed information on how to find Liz. And if it entailed taking a risk and meeting Scott alone…so be it.

Anyway, I thought, gulping down the last of my hot coffee, with dog trainers and punters and race-goers only a hundred yards away, how dangerous could meeting a guy in the car park be? Plus I wouldn't go empty handed. I wasn't that stupid. My brass knuckle duster and trusty double strength hair spray would be part of the weapon cache secreted in my tote bag. Maybe I'd even take along that gray, lifelike water pistol I discovered at Target last month, while buying Lucky a cute purple fluffy dragon toy.

Through the chink in the curtains I could see it was still semi-dark outside. Probably another hour before sunrise. Ben was picking me up in four hours and I had my team of dogs to work plus a trip to the trial track with two breakers before leaving for Port Augusta.

Time to start my day.

I placed my empty plate and cup in the sink and pulled on the warmest coat I owned. A thick sheepskin outback coat that had proven time and time again it was the best defense against the frost and icy wind of a South Australian winter's morning.

"See you later guys," I said to the dogs as I walked through the lounge toward the front door.

My two guard dogs were cuddled together on the sofa. Only Tater's tiny head showed above their thick orange blanket. He opened one eye. Blinked. And then closed it again. The only sign of Lucky was a large immobile orange lump.

"Back door's open for when you need to go out," I told them and pulled on a pair of thick wooly gloves, leaving the two sleeping beauties to their dreams of chasing rabbits and gnawing on dirty old bones.

The ground, white with frost, spread out in every direction. Within two minutes, my nose and cheeks turned to ice and my boots crunched underfoot as I made my way along the dirt path that wound toward the temporary kennel house.

I loved this time of the day. It was as if I was alone in my own little world with no outside nasties to spoil the peace and quiet. No noisy traffic, no soaring electric bills to worry about, no freaking bad guys to send my heart into cardiac arrest. The only sounds in my little world were birds exchanging greetings somewhere high in the trees and oh yeah, a cacophony of barking so loud I expected the roof of the temporary dog shed to lift off and fly away. My greyhounds had heard the front door closing.

By the time Jake arrived two hours later, I'd already worked the racing team and had Zorro and Suzie, the two young breakers, in the back of the station wagon, ready to take them to the trial track.

Jake, his ropy dreadlocks damp, his jeans and T-shirt stained and his eyes red from lack of sleep, dropped his back pack on the floor with a thud and nodded blearily in my direction.

"You look a bit the worse for wear, mate. Been on an all-night drunken binge?"

I grinned at Jake's scowl. I knew he was a health freak and would rather drink rat poison than let a drop of alcohol pass through his body. But it was fun teasing him.

"Yeah, man, been an all-nighter," he agreed propping himself up against the wall. "A baby whale washed up on the beach down South overnight. We only like won the battle to get the poor little guy back with his mama 'bout an hour ago."

"Oh, Jake," I said, guilt washing over me, "why didn't you ring and let me know? I'm covered here. Go home and get some sleep—if you can find the space to lie down in that overcrowded apartment of yours. If not, bunk down in my spare room for a few hours."

Jake's tired smile was ragged around the edges. "You sure, man?"

"Of course I am. I'm almost finished here then I just need to take these two pups to the trial track and I'm outta here," I assured him. "As long as you can take care of the dogs for me tonight. I won't be back from Port Augusta until late."

"Hey, no probs, man."

I had a sudden thought. Saving baby whales was the sort of action Liz thrived on.

"Don't suppose you saw my hippie sister, Liz, on the beach helping out with the baby whale?"

"Nah. Too dark, man. We were like using torches and car headlights and there were masses of people like pushing and pulling and throwing water over the little fellow to keep him alive."

Oh, well. Worth a try. Anyway, Liz probably wouldn't leave her old friend, the endangered tree, in case the bulldozers snuck in while she was away saving the marine life.

My mind switched back to Scott's text. *L in trouble*. I sighed. Hopefully it was just tree-saving trouble. The sort of trouble associated with delayed bulldozers and axes and not the sort of trouble that could leave her lifeless and covered in ice, body jammed inside a refrigerator.

*****

Stiff and tired after a long, boring, three hour drive along the A1 highway to Port Augusta, I let out a sigh of relief as Ben maneuvered his four wheel drive and dog trailer into the inner car park at Chinnery Park, and slowed to a halt. Port Augusta. A city advertised on most travel brochures as the 'gateway to the Flinders Ranges. The seaport and railway junction city located on the east coast of the Eyre Peninsula'. But to us, one of the friendliest country greyhound tracks in South Australia.

Ben pocketed his car keys and lifted the lid on the tack box at the front of the trailer. "Here, you take the dogs on that side," he said passing me two leads and muzzles. "I'll get these three."

With half an hour to kennel closing we walked the dogs around the outer circumference of the track, allowing them to stretch their legs, sniff, and empty out before being confined in the kennel house. Then, while Ben prepared his dog for the first race, I wandered across to the betting ring. Used to be a dozen bookies at this track, all enticing punters to donate their money to their worthy cause, but times change and now there were only two.

I approached Big Mick, a familiar bookie I'd had dealings with before. Due to a misunderstanding, there was little love lost between us. At the time, I'd mistakenly thought the burly bookie was involved in a betting scam and while visiting his home, accused him of the crime. Let's say he didn't take well to accusations. Anyway, even though it turned out he wasn't the brains behind the scam, I still wouldn't put it past him to be in the middle of anything dodgy.

"Hi Mick, how's the family?" I asked plastering a smile on my face.

Mick cast his eyes away from setting up prices for the first race and scowled. "Oh, it's you."

"Triplets doing well?" I persisted, cementing my smile in place, even adding a touch of animation to my voice. Geez. The things a sleuth has to do to wrangle information from a source. "And what about those gorgeous twins of yours?" I went on, in full acting mode. "Little Eddy still throwing everything he can grab hold of? Wouldn't be surprised if Junior makes the Australian baseball team when he grows up."

The reason I knew about Junior's good right arm came from experience. Several well-aimed clumps of spaghetti, plus a spoon that hit their target—my face—the day I'd called in for a visit. The day I'd discovered Big Mick, of the beer gut, receding hair line and wet gooby lips, had fathered seven kids all under the age of seven.

Immediately Mick thawed. Guess it was the proud father syndrome. "Yeah, yeah, kids all doing well, thanks. Little Eddy has progressed from tossing spaghetti. The little bugger threw a chair at me last week."

Good for Little Eddy. But I vowed to keep all future interrogations with Mick to the race track and well away from his over stimulated offspring.

"Lately, I've heard rumors," I said and nudged my tote bag into a more comfortable position on my shoulder. A position where I'd have easy access to knuckle duster, hair spray and/or water pistol, if needed. "Rumors about unusual things happening at country tracks. Have *you* heard anything about that, Mick?"

His scowl returned—in spades. "What are you accusing me of *this* time?"

"Nothing," I gave a dismissive shrug. "Just heard on the grape vine there'd been some rumbles of discontent at the country tracks lately. Thought you might know something about it."

"Well, you thought wrong."

Mick's bagman, a skinny guy in thick bifocal glasses, leant forward. "Do you mean slow dogs winning at huge odds yet not turning up anything illegal in their swabs?"

My ears pricked. Aha, so that's what Scott was referring to. "Er…yeah," I moved closer, all the better to prod the guy into revealing more. "What do you make of that?"

"He makes nothing of that," snapped Mick and shoved a clipboard in the direction of his bagman's stomach. "In fact if he doesn't stop yakking and get to work, the first race will be over before we can lay a bet."

"Did you lose money when the slow dogs won, Mick? Or did you get a tip-off and make yourself a profit?"

All I got for that question was a stiff finger, so, realizing the conversation was over I sauntered across to the catching pen to catch Ben's dog in the first race.

Ben's dog, Vanilla Gorilla, won by six lengths and as Ben didn't have a runner in the second race we decided to eat lunch at the cafeteria. A whopping plate of fish and chips with lashings of salad. The fish caught locally and melt-in-the mouth tasty.

While Ben inhaled the food as though he hadn't eaten for a month, I took a breath now and then to quiz anyone passing by about whether they'd seen Liz. It wasn't until we'd almost finished our meal that I scored a hit. A pleasant faced lady of indeterminate age, wearing a long flowery dress and a fringed shawl, large hooped earrings and a rainbow hued scarf around her head introduced herself as Lady Margaret. She said she ran the local craft shop in Port Augusta West and that a young woman answering to Liz's description had dropped in a few times to buy raffia. According to the lady from the craft shop, the young woman was making sleeping baskets for stray dogs at the pound.

I sighed. Yep. That would be my little sister. "Did she mention where she was living?"

"Can't say she did, dear."

"It's important."

"Well…not to me she didn't…but Old Sal, the butcher on Commercial Road, he told Mrs. Papadopoulos, my friend who runs the Greek restaurant next door to him, that when he were delivering meat to one of his out-of-town customers, he'd seen this young woman in shorts, and not much else, outside a deserted rabbiter's shack. She were like sitting cross legged in the dirt and having a conversation with the sky."

Ignoring the expression on the woman's face that clearly said even Lady Margaret of the fringed shawl and hooped earrings thought this behavior a bit off-putting, I placed a hand on her arm to stop her from moving on. "Just before you go, when was the last time my sister came into your shop?"

"Oh, let's see, only last week. Yes, it were a Thursday. I remember 'cos the little lady said it were her birthday. Said she were going to treat herself with a gluten-free cupcake from the bakery."

Now I felt guilty. Of course it was Liz's birthday last Thursday. My little sister had turned twenty-one and it sounded like she'd partied on a lousy cupcake—alone.

"I asked her if she were going out with her boyfriend that night? You know, for her birthday. Said they'd broken up and men were slimy worms and couldn't be trusted."

So Scott was lying to me about their current relationship. What other lies had he fed me?

Beside me, Ben looked at the clock on the cafeteria wall, pushed his well-polished plate aside and got to his feet. "I'll see you in the catching pen, Kat. Okay?"

I gave him a quick wave and thumbs up for luck in the next race, then turned back to the craft shop owner. "Sorry to hold you up," I said. "But did my sister seem scared or upset that day?"

"Now you mention it, she did seem a bit agitated. Kept looking over her shoulder. I asked her if she were meeting someone and she said no, just in a hurry."

"Did you notice if there was anyone suspicious hanging around?"

"Couple of youngsters who should have been in school but they were just out the front playing on their phones. And—oh yeah, I did see an elderly gentleman. He was one of those who were like, mutton done up as lamb. You know, dark sunglasses, stomach hanging under a tight fitting shirt and these dazzling yellow trousers that made me blink. Remember thinking how ridiculous he looked. Anyway, I gave your sister some pretty silver baubles to sew on her skirt, seeing it were her birthday, and she left."

Sounded like Jack Lantana had been hanging around in front of the craft shop. Had he kidnapped Liz? Was that how her bracelet ended up in his house? Or had Liz merely lost the bracelet in the street and Jack picked it up?

"The old guy? Did he follow her?"

"Sorry, dear, I don't know what happened to the elderly gent," she said and shook her head. "And now, I must go. My son, Wayne, has a dog in the next race and he asked me to put a few dollars on for him. Dog's called Sizzler. Should be 50/1 but knowing how miserly those two money-sucking bookies are, I'll be lucky if they put the dog up at 10's."

Leaving Lady Margaret to do battle with the bookies, I bought myself a country-baked vanilla slice. The biggest, mouth-watering vanilla slice I'd ever laid eyes on. Then, cake clutched in both hands, face sticky with creamy custard—not the chewy rubbery custard found in store-bought slices—I wandered over to the catching pen in readiness to catch Ben's dog at the finish of the race. As I walked, I churned over the new information I'd learned about Liz.

She'd been shopping in Port Augusta last Thursday, so definitely wasn't missing then. Some*thing* or some*one* made her nervous that day. An old guy in yellow pants was spotted hanging around in front of the craft shop while she was inside.

And Liz had already broken up with Scott Brady.

17

I was glad i'd worn my thick sheepskin coat to the track. The afternoon sky had turned gunmetal gray, while gathering nimbus clouds forecast rain, and a cold blustery wind had spectators more inclined to watch the races on the big screen television under cover of the betting ring. The die-hards who liked to view their races live hung over the outside railing, colorful in their coats, scarves and wooly hats.

Ben won the Maiden race over 447meters with a handy youngster whose clown of an owner had named the dog, *Wimpy Wally*. Luckily the name didn't affect the dog's ability, although it gave the race caller a good laugh. Lady Margaret's son Wayne's dog, *Sizzler*, was—as they say in racing jargon—'still-coming'.

As Ben had two greyhounds engaged in the fifth race, he rugged up a cheeky little white and black bitch with the racing name of *Better Be Good,* while I handled her litter sister, *She's a Good Girl*. Most races on the program were over 447 or 503 meters but this race was over the longer distance of 682. Bred from strong staying lines, both Ben's bitches, known at home as Molly and Polly, were already proven over the longer journey and I wasn't surprised to find the bookies opening them up as short equal favorites to win.

"Hold still, Molly," I implored as I slipped the number three—a white rug—over her head, eased the front legs through their respective holes and slid the silky lycra material along her back. I could see Ben having similar problems with Polly. She reminded me of a toddler having a tantrum. While Ben endeavored to straighten the red rug, number one, over her body, before leading the runners out of the kennel house into the parade ring, she refused to stand still.

Molly, eager to get out onto the track, bounced up and down. Knowing her tendency to leap high in the air and throw herself over backwards if allowed on the end of the lead, I kept her close to my side while parading. "Easy, girl. Not long now."

On the long drive to Port Augusta, while flicking through the race book, I'd noticed a dog called, *Go Rambo* entered in this race. I'd previously trained Rambo and was surprised to see the dog entered in a staying race. When I trained him he could barely stagger over the line in a sprint. A gangly black dog with the heart of a marshmallow, Rambo was such a loving dog, always ready to lick your face and lap up attention, but slow as the proverbial tortoise on the race track. At the time I'd tried to talk the owner into placing Rambo into the GAP program because of the dog's gorgeous temperament, but the owner decided to send him to a trainer up north. Probably figured it was easier to win a race in the country.

Hand resting on Molly's head to keep her calm, I glanced around at the other runners. Rambo must be the big black dog in the pink rug on the opposite side of the parade ring. The handler, a tall skinny guy with a ponytail leaned against the fence, his eyes on the nearby betting ring. Evidently couldn't be bothered walking the dog to stretch its legs and warm its muscles before the race. Didn't he realize cold muscles tore more easily?

"G'day," I said moving up alongside the pair. "I'm Kat McKinley. I know Rambo—used to train the big softy." I stretched one hand out to fondle Rambo's ears. The big sook loved his ears rubbed—always sent him into a tail wagging frenzy. "How you doing, big boy?" I frowned. The dog's tail didn't move. Instead, he turned his head away, ignoring me—almost like he didn't know me.

With a snarl, Ponytail snatched the dog away. "Get ya hands off me dog or I'll call the steward."

"Sorry," I said and took a step back, surprised at the man's aggression. I could see Ben scowling from the other side of the parade ring and not wanting to cause a scene, continued walking. When I looked over my shoulder, Ponytail had gone back to his original position—his slack body holding up the fence, eyes trained on the betting ring. There was something familiar about Ponytail, but I couldn't figure out where I'd seen him before.

"What was *that* all about?" Ben, white handlers' coat stretched across his rugged chest, emphasizing the hard six pack underneath, brought Polly up beside me. "Want me to go over and deck that creep for you?"

"Hey, my fault. I shouldn't have touched another trainer's dog," I said, placing a warning hand on Ben's arm. "But it's Rambo. Remember that gorgeous snail of a dog I used to have in my kennels? The one who was forever trying to sit in my lap? Well, I just tried to say hello to him but the dog seems to have forgotten me."

"Sure it's Rambo?"

"Yep. *Go Rambo*. He's entered in this race."

Ben shook his head. "But that dog can't even run out a sprint race. Why would they enter him in a staying race?"

"Beats me. But if he's no stronger than he was when I had him, they'll be scraping poor Rambo off the dirt half way through the race."

At that moment, the steward called all runners to line up in box order in front of the gate ready to parade onto the race-track.

Trailing behind the number two dog, I led Molly through the gate and onto the track toward the starting boxes, my shoes sinking into the grass surface. Off to the west and south-west, I could see a range of hills which once marked the territory of the Nukunu Aboriginal tribe, and all around, the age-old hulk of the Flinders Ranges, a dark, sprawling shadow against the vast canopy of a gray winter's sky.

Two minutes later, the hum of the bramich lure powering around the track sent the eight-dog field barking and scratching at the grating in front of their respective boxes. And the instant the lids sprung open Ben's two greyhounds jumped to the lead. Neck and neck they galloped around the track. I glanced back through the runners, worried about Rambo. No need. He was galloping strongly in the middle of the field. As the dogs swung into the home straight, it was Polly by a nose, then Molly, but out of the pack, running past his competitors as though they'd been nailed to the fence, came a big black dog—*Go Rambo*. The dog that couldn't run out a 400 meter race whipped passed Ben's two stayers and went on to win the 648 metre race by three lengths.

I stood behind the boxes, mouth in fly-catching mode, collar and lead forgotten at my feet. Holy crap! What amazing additives was this new trainer feeding the dog? What was his secret training regime? Or had I just witnessed a miracle akin to the parting of the Red Sea? Here was a greyhound who'd finished last in his previous fourteen race starts— winning the distance race at 50/1 and beating two proven city performers.

Big Mick's bagman's words about what was happening at the country tracks passed through my head:…*slow dogs winning at huge odds yet not turning up anything illegal in their swabs…*

Was Rambo one of these dogs?

While I removed Molly's race rug and washed her feet at the hose bay, I noticed a steward accompanying Ponytail and the prancing Rambo toward the Swab Box. Prancing? How could this be the same dog? In the past, Rambo would lie down on the track after his race and refuse to move. Nine times out of ten I'd had to carry the exhausted dog back to the kennel house.

As Ponytail swaggered past toward the Swab Box, he gave me a sly wink. "If ya need any tips on training those slow pooches of yours— come see me."

"Not if you were the last trainer on Earth."

His crooked grin didn't match the venom in his eyes.

It was when Ponytail turned his back and followed the track vet outside to collect a sample of urine for the swab tests from Rambo that I finally remembered where I'd seen the man before. Tall and skinny. Long greasy strawberry blonde pony-tailed hair, red socks and scuffed brown shoes. It was the same guy I'd seen arguing with Gina. She'd called him Garry.

What had Garry been doing in Gina's barn? Was he responsible for stealing Stanley—and if so, why? And was I wrong about my friend, Gina? Was she somehow involved in this shady betting scam too?

Before I could contemplate any of these questions, I needed to psyche myself up to go meet Scott Brady. Thankfully, Ben had a runner engaged in the sixth race so as soon as I'd arranged for someone else to catch Ben's dog, I set off for the outside car park. Not having any idea what Liz's ex-boyfriend looked like, I could have already bumped into him on the track. In fact, Scott could have been trailing me all afternoon. Watching me scratch that recurring itch on my left buttock. Rolling his eyes when I smeared my face with vanilla custard. Or maybe he'd come close enough to cutting me with his knife and chickened out when Ben appeared.

I let out a sigh. Was I being foolish meeting this guy on my own? Of course I was. But how else could I find out more about my missing sister?

Tote bag hitched high on my shoulder, knuckle duster in one coat pocket and a can of *Ubeaut* extra-strong hair spray tucked in the other, I scanned the car park for a red VW Beetle. Most trainers and patrons preferred to drive onto the Chinnery Park grounds and park around the track so it was easy to spot the beat up red Beetle, parked on its own, in the far corner of the outside car park, partly hidden by two large jacaranda bushes. I remember reading a book called *Mind Hunter*, written by the professional profiler, John Douglas. In it, he proclaimed VW Beetles seemed to be the car of choice for most serial killers.

My bravado did a nose dive and my long purposeful strides faltered, switched to a shuffle. Why did my traitorous mind have to dredge up that chilling piece of information while my reluctant body was making its way toward an assignation with a man who DI Adams claimed had been 'put away' for assault?

In the distance I heard a loudspeaker crackle and the on-course race-caller inform punters that betting for race six would close in thirty seconds. This was followed by the sound of metal doors clanging. If I didn't get a move on race six would be over and Ben would be out looking for me. So when an icy wind blew strands of hair across my face, I shivered, tugged my coat collar up around my ears and hurried toward the red Beetle hunched like a giant bug on the far side of the car park. No young man leaning against the bonnet, waiting for me. Not a soul in sight. Was Scott playing hide-go-seek? If he'd set out to deliberately scare me—his plan was working.

I tightened my fingers around the can of hair spray in my pocket. If this man was playing games with me and he had no knowledge of where I could find Liz, I'd let him have it—a stinging spray full in the face. Hey, I was tired of being pushed around by crappy crooks.

As I drew closer, the monotonous sound of the Beetle's idling motor brought me to a halt. Surely Scott wasn't planning to hit me over the head, drag me into his vehicle and drive off? I frowned, peered at the car more closely and felt my stomach roil. Something was terribly wrong with this picture. All the VW's windows were shut and fogged up. A hose pipe, duct taped in place, had been fed into the driver's side window, the gap each side plugged with what looked like old rags. I ran my eye from the window to the end of the hose…it was jammed into the car's exhaust pipe.

"Nooooo!"

Heart thumping louder than blocked drains in an outdated bathroom, I bolted across the bitumen and past the bushes, couldn't see through the car's fogged up windows, so tugged frantically at the door handle.

"Don't be dead! *Don't* you *dare* be dead!" I yelled at the young man aged in his early twenties and dressed in khaki chinos and a tan leather jacket who spilled out of the car, his head, complete with collar-length dark hair streaked with blonde, bouncing off the ground as he landed.

The young man didn't seem to be paying attention, so, coughing and retching as the deadly carbon monoxide flooded my lungs, I covered my mouth with one hand and reached inside the car to turn off the ignition.

"Scott! Scott! Can you hear me?"

No reaction and his chest didn't seem to be moving. Shit. Digging into my tote-bag I dragged out my phone. After dialing 911, I dragged

Scott's limp body further from the car's toxic fumes then knelt over him. Should I give him the kiss of life? Or wait until the medics arrived.

I decided to give it a go and placed one hand, heel down on the lower half of his breast bone then placed the other hand on top and intertwined my fingers. Now, what was it? Thirty compressions—then two breaths into the mouth? Or was it twenty compressions—then five breaths into the mouth? Oh God, I should have paid more attention when we were taught CPR in high school instead of giggling at Tanya who poked her tongue out every time she pushed down on the dummy's chest.

One-two-three-four…

Why would a young man with his life before him commit suicide? And why do it in such a public place? Surely it would have been more comfortable to set this up in his garage. Perhaps there was no garage where he was living or he was afraid the other tenants might wander in and succumb to the toxic fumes. Or perhaps this was a one-man public protest against the culling of koalas or the rising cost of electricity that had gone too far.

I could hear the muffled wail of sirens in the far distance and strengthened my compressions.

Twenty-five…twenty-six…twenty-seven…

I studied the young man's face, pink from inhaling carbon monoxide poisoning. His ocean blue eyes stared back at me, wide and unseeing. A cold shiver jerked in the pit of my stomach, raced up into my chest and from there into my limbs.

Scott Brady, my sister's ex-boyfriend, was either in a dead coma—or just plain dead.

18

Big fat drops of rain blasted my face, blurring my vision. They slid into my open mouth and stuck my wispy hair to my forehead in clinging saturated strands. By the time two police cars and an ambulance screamed through the gate and pulled up beside me, I was kneeling in a puddle of water. A miserable soggy mass of reluctant rescuer—still pumping—still counting compressions—and wishing the hell for a tent, an umbrella or even a plastic bag to cover my head. Without warning, the heavens had flung their pearly gates open and tossed another obstacle in my path—a rating ten rain squall.

I looked up, as, equipment in tow, two medics, a voluptuous redhead and a grandfatherly looking guy with the name GRANT pinned to his uniform, leaped from the front cab of the ambulance and bustled over.

"Okay, love, we'll take over now," said the grandfatherly guy, easing me out of the way before continuing with CPR.

"Be my guest," I said and let out a sigh, more than happy to hand over Scott's resuscitating procedure to the experts. My legs, cramped from kneeling, went a bit wobbly as I stood up. Hunched over, I wiped rain from my eyes and hobbled across to huddle under the shelter of the nearby bushes.

"Did you get any response at all?" called out the voluptuous redhead inserting a needle into Scott's arm while her partner continued counting out compressions.

"Could be my imagination, but I thought he blinked his eyes when you pulled into the car park."

"Good."

I stayed where I was, hunched over, coat collar pulled up, eyes glued to Scott's pink face, praying the medics would succeed where I had failed.

"He took a breath!" The guy called Grant gasped, renewing his efforts. "Quick. Have the oxygen ready."

I stepped closer, eager to witness a miracle. And when Scott started coughing and spluttering, causing Grant to finally cease CPR and slide an oxygen mask over the patient's face, I punched the air with my fist. Let out a throaty, *Yeeees!* Okay, I didn't actually *know* Liz's ex-boyfriend, but after exchanging mouth fluids while giving a person the kiss of life, it's only natural to form a close attachment. In fact I had to mentally restrain myself from doing a tap dance in the nearest puddle—for fear my version of 'Singing in the Rain' might plummet the patient into another coma.

As they stabilized and loaded Scott into the ambulance, Grant smiled across at me. "Whoever this man is—he owes his life to you, young lady. Good work."

I smiled back, then, suddenly deflated, shook my head. "Maybe he won't thank me when he wakes up. Maybe he'll just be angry I pulled him from the car."

"Suicide is a strange thing," Grant said, climbing into the driver's seat. "When he realizes how close he came to not being here, he'll feel differently. Don't worry."

I could see two young police constables near Scott's VW Beetle while three other uniforms kept bug-eyed spectators from getting any closer.

The only other policeman, an ox of a man built like a linebacker, seemed to be in charge of the scene. Like the others, he was dressed in the traditional country uniform of khaki trousers, RM Williams drizabone over khaki shirt and a khaki colored Akubra hat with a blue and white checked band. After snapping orders like bullets at the men near Scott's car, he turned toward me. Back ramrod straight, he marched across the bitumen.

"Name?" he barked.

I drew myself up to my full height, which meant the tip of my nose reached his breastbone, tilted my head back, and scowled up at him. Ever since I'd run up against Miss Emily Virgo, an officious teacher in sixth grade who bullied instead of encouraging her pupils, I'd rebelled against that tone of voice. Okay, it had got me into the headmaster's office a few times but that only made me rebel more politely.

"Sorry, but if *you* don't know your name—neither do I."

His frown imploded in on itself. I could see impatience and a flick of surprise spark in his eyes. He sniffed and shifted his weight back on his heels. "I'm Senior Constable Mark Kelly, the constable in charge of this operation."

"And I'm Kat McKinley," I said and thrust out my hand, which he ignored. Instead he switched on a small recorder, his eyes never leaving mine. Returning the glare, I withdrew my hand and stuffed it into my soggy coat pocket. "In fact," I continued in my best *hey-you!* voice, "*I'm* the lady you should be putting up for a medal, instead of treating like a criminal."

His face reddened and one hand strayed to his accoutrement belt, where a gun, radio, some sort of spray, handcuffs and a retractable baton lurked. "You can either answer my questions here or down at the station."

His steely gaze continued to bore through me until I lowered my eyes to his muddy black RM Williams boots. Okay, maybe this was different from standing up to bossy Miss Virgo. She might have carried an athletic ruler but she sure as heck didn't pack a gun.

"Here is fine."

His lips flattened in what could be interpreted as a triumphant smile—or the effects of indigestion. "Ms McKinley, are you acquainted with the man who attempted to commit suicide?"

"Sorry, don't know him from Adam," I said and shook my head. Okay…sort of the truth. I didn't actually *know* him. Only knew *of* him. Couldn't even be sure the guy in the car *was* Scott Brady.

"So, tell me, what exactly were you doing out here? Is this where you parked your car?"

"No. I was just—going for a walk. You know, stretching my legs."

"In the rain?"

"It wasn't raining then." I scowled. "Now, Senior Constable Kelly, do you want me to answer your question or not?"

"Continue."

"Thank you. I was going for a walk, stretching my legs—"

"As you've already informed me."

"—when I spotted this red car partly hidden behind the bushes," I said ignoring his rudeness. "And of course when I saw a hose leading from the passenger window into the exhaust, I immediately switched off the ignition, rang for help, and pulled the victim from the car." I gave him one of my most beatific smiles. "As any like-minded citizen in the same situation would do."

Hey, I wasn't fool enough to let this gnarly policeman know I'd been on my way to a pre-arranged meeting with Scott when I spotted his car set up as a weapon of destruction. Until I knew what was going on, this information wasn't an option.

"Senior Constable," one of the policemen called out, interrupting the interview. The constable had a sort of breathing apparatus covering his face and came hurrying from the direction of the red Beetle, holding a sheet of paper at one corner by the tips of his gloved fingers. "Found a suicide note. The man's name is Scott Brady and he's confessed to killing some guy down in Adelaide by the name of Jack Lantana."

Whaaaat?

I swear my ears stood up and waggled. Why would Scott kill Jack? How did he even know Jack? And where did my sister fit into all this?

"Bag it," ordered Kelly, rubbing his hands together and growing an extra couple of inches in height. "And after notifying the CSI and the

PES make sure two uniforms are assigned to take turns guarding the offender while he's in hospital." He turned back to me, his chest expanding in correlation with the importance of the criminal found on his patch. "You may go now, Ms. McKinley, but I want you to come down to the station at your earliest convenience and sign a statement." Then, without waiting for my acquiescence, he left me huddled under the bushes and strode away, presumably to intimidate another likely victim.

Soaked to the skin, confused, and determined to stay in Port Augusta until Scott woke up then somehow slip past a vigilant policeman at the hospital so I could get some answers about Liz, I went to find Ben.

I had to let him know he'd be going home without me.

*****

"No way. If you're staying here in Port Augusta—so am I."

"But you can't. What about your dogs?"

Ben placed his hands on my shoulders and began to knead the muscles with the tips of his fingers. Felt good. So good I almost let go and started blubbing. "Don't worry, babe. We'll book a hotel room for the night and I'll ask Kenny Gilbert to put my dogs up. He's a good mate."

"Oh Ben, what's going on?" I shivered and it wasn't just from wearing wet clothes. "I can't believe Scott would kill the old guy who was stealing my dogs. Why would he? Scott sounded scared when he spoke to me on the phone. Or do you think he was just playing me for a fool?"

Ben pulled me up against him. "If he *was* then I hope the mongrel gets what he deserves. If not… I'm glad you were there to save his life."

"And what about Liz? Where the heck is *she*? Fair dinkum, I'm going to wring her stubborn little neck when I find her. Make her promise to contact me every week. Let me know where she is and what she's up to." I took a breath. Met Ben's eyes. "Ben, I didn't tell you this before because I thought you'd get upset, but Scott sent me a text yesterday. He asked me to meet him here and said Liz was in trouble."

Ben's fingers on my shoulders stilled. "You should have told me, babe."

"I know, I know. I'm sorry. But I thought you'd get all, *me-Tarzan-you-Jane,* and insist on coming with me and Scott said to come alone."

"And since when have *you* ever followed orders?"

I sniffed. Let that one ride. "Anyway, that's why I have to talk to Scott now—find out what he knows about Liz." And then a staggering thought hit me. Punched me like a fist in the chest. Made me gasp. "Oh, Jesus, what if Scott killed Liz before attempting to commit suicide? What if I just saved the monster that killed my sister?"

A convulsive full body shiver took hold of me leaving me barely able to stand. Loud background noises dimmed. The frenetic barking of dogs and shouts of trainers preparing to leave the course were replaced by a strange humming noise in my ears. I closed my eyes and clung onto Ben's shirt like a life support in a raging sea.

"Easy does it, darling." Ben's arms, reassuring and rock solid pulled me against him and his voice crooned in my ear. "Don't go trying to second guess this thing, babe, 'cos that's the way madness lies." He bent to entwine his fingers into a handful of my wet straggly hair, eased my face up to his and the gentle kiss that followed kick-started my brain, sent blood pounding through my body again. "Don't worry. We'll find a way to talk to Scott and question him about Liz. Even if I have to dress up as a bloody nurse and threaten to bash the guy on the head with a bedpan. Okay?"

I nodded. The vision of a 6'3" nurse built to play ruck in a weekend footy match, mincing into the hospital room carrying a lethal bedpan made me smile.

"Now," Ben went on, evidently happy to see the smile. "Let's get these dogs settled so we can find somewhere to shower and change into dry clothes before going to the hospital to visit a…sick friend."

After ringing and organizing for Jake to take over my team for twenty-four hours and Ben's brother, Nick, to look after the dogs he'd left at home, we went to find Kenny Gilbert.

"Sure can, mate," said Kenny when Ben asked to leave his dogs in his kennels overnight. "Just follow me home and we'll shift a few dogs around. Make some room." He gazed at me with sympathetic eyes. "You okay, Kat? Must have been a shock to find young Scott Brady trying to top himself in the car park."

I looked up. "You know Scott?"

"Sure. The guy could be a bit of a dickhead at times but he's been helping out at the track lately and doin' a great job. You know, cleaning out the kennel-house, taking money at the gate, grading the track on trial days, stuff like that. Can't believe he'd want to do 'imself in though. Always seemed happy enough to me."

This was too good an opportunity to miss. "Did he have a girlfriend?"

"Can't say I know much about his love life," Kenny said closing the van door after his two greyhounds had leapt inside and settled down on the mattress for their ride home. "But come to think of it, he did bring a good looking chick to the track a few times. Bit of a hippy by the looks of her. You know, long dress, scarves, a shitload of beads dangling around her neck. Wasn't really welcome here though. She kept waving this silly placard under our noses—protesting about forcing greyhounds to run, or some such rubbish. Told the silly bird there was no way anyone could *make* a dog run if he didn't want to. No jockey on top makin' him go, is there? But of course, she didn't listen. That sort never do."

Yep. That was my sister, Liz. "So…when was the last time you saw her?"

Kenny shrugged. "Hmm…just over a week ago. I remember Bob Germaine having a right go at her. He's the guy they sent up from Adelaide to stand in for our club secretary who's in hospital having knee surgery. I was too far away to hear the argument but I can imagine Bob told her to stick her stupid placard where the sun don't shine. Anyway, I haven't seen the bird here since."

Kenny climbed into the front seat of his van, slammed the door and shouted across to Ben who'd parked next to him, ready to follow his mate home. "Hey, bro, lost a couple hundred bucks when that snail *Go Rambo* beat your two bitches today. Couldn't believe my eyes. Dog's normally slower than salary rises. In fact, I reckon my three legged Labrador could beat *Go Rambo* with his back legs tied together."

Ben nodded. "Sure didn't look like the same dog I'd seen racing down the city and finishing so far behind the rest of the field it looked like he was taking part in a separate race."

"Beats me what's going on, mate. There's been some bloody strange results at the country tracks lately," Ken told us. "Yet, you'll see, like the other slow dogs that won, *Go Rambo's* swab will come back negative."

Kenny turned the key in his ignition while I slid in beside Ben and we followed the white van around the outside of the track toward the gateway leading onto the main highway.

As we drove through the outside car park I looked across at the little red Beetle partially hidden by the jacaranda bushes. The police were still there, milling around the car, checking inside and out, taking photos, dusting for fingerprints. And as we passed under the arch that rose above the front gate, a big black car pulled in. The car looked very official and I could see two suited men sitting in the front seat. Unsmiling, poker faced.

Looked like the Big Brass had arrived.

19

It was ten o'clock the following morning. Slivers of hesitant sunlight poked around the edges of the clouds as I inhaled a deep breath of cool air, held it for ten, and then blew the air in Ben's direction. Together, we stood, hovering, outside the Port Augusta hospital, rested and changed—but with no viable plan of action.

"You know, I still think my idea of offering the guard a chocolate, laced with sleeping pills, would work."

"Yep. Probably would," Ben replied reaching out with one large hand to gently push hair from my eyes, "but jail time is not featured in our plans for the future, babe."

Our and *future*.

Warm prickles scurried across my skin and I had a sudden urge to slip both hands under Ben's chocolate brown polo shirt, the one that mirrored the color of his eyes, and show him exactly what *I* thought of those two lovely words together in one sentence.

Down girl! I gulped another deep fortifying breath of cold air and stared at the plain brickwork of the hospital, silently counting windows in an attempt to distract my wanton thoughts. "Well, it's better than *your* wacky idea," I growled. "You know, the one where I do a strip-tease in the passageway while you sneak past the cop on duty into Scott Brady's room."

Ben quirked one eyebrow, a cheeky grin crinkling his lips. "You're probably right. I'd want to stay and watch the show too—see how far you'd go to distract the guard."

"*Duh*. As if I'd even start."

On our approach, the automatic glass doors whirred open allowing a gang of leather clad bikers, most with blackened eyes or white bandages wrapped around their skull, to exit. After sucking one last gasp of fresh air, I followed Ben inside. As soon as the glass doors closed, my irrational fear of hospitals took over—artificial air, sick people, and the chilling smell of strong disinfectant and pain. An ice cold lump settled in my stomach and instant sweat blossomed under my armpits.

Not so Ben. He strode purposely toward the enquiry desk. To keep up with him I had to push my fears aside and lengthen my stride, our footsteps echoing on the hospital issue gray tiled floor as we walked.

"This is madness. Like reporting for an exam on molecular structure without knowing the first thing about physics," I said. "Ben, we have no plan to get past the uniform on duty outside Scott's door. We need one."

"What say we try the legitimate way first? Ask if Scott's allowed visitors. If not, we'll play up the fact that you're the lovely lady who rescued him and you just *have* to see if the poor man is okay."

"Hmmm…worth a try," I agreed. The sooner I spoke to Scott the sooner I'd find Liz.

We followed more signs on walls, and traipsed along what felt like several hundred passageways until we came to the Psychiatric ward.

Now came the tricky part.

"Good morning, I'm Kat McKinley," I told a stressed looking nurse sitting behind the front desk. "I've come to visit Scott Brady."

"Sorry," she said, a frown creasing her forehead. "No-one's allowed in with Mr. Brady. He's under police guard and suicide watch."

"Been a hectic morning, has it?" said Ben leaning his frame against the counter and aiming his hundred watt smile at the nurse. "Not that you look flustered. You look cool headed and serene. Like that movie star in *Sabrina*."

She didn't even glance up, just continued pecking away on the computer keyboard.

Ben's smile fizzled to a lowly 25 watts while I couldn't prevent a muffled giggle. Benjamin Taylor considered himself the ultimate lady's man and was always surprised when his obvious flirting didn't hit pay dirt. However, as his girlfriend, I found his failures quite satisfying to witness.

The other nurse at the desk glanced up from writing a report, caught Ben's dimming smile and immediately blotted her lipstick between her full lips. "Yes, it *has* been chaotic this morning—but all part of a day's work. What can I do for you, sir?"

Ben's smile lifted its game and zoomed in on nurse number two who was definitely more receptive to his charms. "I'm Ben Taylor and this is Kat McKinley and you're—" he paused, eyeing the name tag pinned to her starched uniform. "—Belinda Tanner. Well, Belinda, we were hoping to see a patient. Scott Brady."

With another blot of her lipstick and a large smile for Ben, she turned to me. "Kat McKinley? Aren't you the lady who pulled Mr. Brady from his car yesterday?"

"Yes, that's the reason I want to see him," I said, putting on a long face together with big puppy dog eyes. "I've been thinking of the poor man all night."

"Actually, Mr. Brady's been asking to see you. We've been worried about his recovery because he's upset and won't settle down. Says he needs to thank you."

"He does?"

"Yes." Once again the nurse's eyes settled on Ben and she slipped him a wink. *Damn hussy*. Still, if it got us through Scott's door, I guess I could refrain from strangling the woman with a dog lead—this time. "If you'd like to wait here, I'll have a word with the cop on duty," she said. "Officer Joel Patterson and I were in the same class at primary school, so maybe I can talk him into letting you in to see our patient."

She paused for effect, this time with a roll of her eyes. "Especially if I emphasize the fact that I spotted him cuddling a blonde bird, dressed in little more than a brightly colored scarf, deep in a dark corner of the Sunset Lagoon nightclub last weekend. And the woman he was cuddling was *not* raven-haired, Suzy, his current girlfriend."

With another wink at Ben, the nurse set off down the passageway, emphasizing the *kaboom-kaboom* of her booty with every measured step.

"Earth to Ben," I said and dug a well sharpened elbow into his ribs. "By the drool running down your chin, you're enjoying that display far too much."

Nurse Belinda spoke to the policeman on duty and within a couple of minutes she looked back at us and waved. "He says it's okay, you can go in for a few minutes, Kat—but your *friend* will have to wait outside."

"Go on," said Ben, pushing me forward. "I'll keep my ear to the door, in case you need a distraction."

"As long as that's *all* you do while I'm otherwise engaged," I warned.

Officer Patterson stood up from his sentry's chair as I approached. "I'm going against direct orders here," he said. "But I saw you at the greyhound track yesterday struggling to keep the guy in there alive. I'll give you three minutes to talk to him but you can't talk about the case and I'll be standing beside the suspect's bed the whole time. Orders you know."

"Thank you, Officer." *Damn.* How could I grill Scott with a uniform hanging on every word I spoke? Shrugging my shoulders at Ben, I followed Officer Patterson through the doorway into a single hospital room and looked around. The patient was propped up in bed and although he'd lost his scary pink coloring and seemed to be breathing a little easier, he certainly didn't look ready for a night on the town yet.

"Hi Scott," I said, smiling as I approached the bed. "I'm Kat McKinley. How are you feeling today?"

He didn't return the smile. "I feel like someone who's woken up after being given a drink laced with drugs only to find they've been bundled into their own car and they're the victim of an attempted murder."

My ears almost stood up and wiggled. "Yeah? Is that what happened?"

Officer Patterson grunted. "Mr. Brady, please restrict your conversation to the weather or other neutral topics or Ms. McKinley will have to leave."

Crap.

Scott lifted his chin at me and sniffed. "'Spose I've got *you* to thank for me being alive."

What a sweetheart. Not. "'Spose you do." I twisted a strand of my hair and glanced across at the policeman on the other side of the bed. The uniform stood soldier straight, arms crossed, face impassive.

"So…Scott…has your *girlfriend* been in to see you yet?"

"Haven't got a girlfriend."

So that's how he was going to play it. Like a clam. I should have left the little toad to turn into a pink Popsicle. "Come on, a good looking guy like you must have a girlfriend."

"Girlfriend's indisposed."

"Why's that? Where is she?"

"I'm sorry, Ms. McKinley, I'll have to ask you to leave. I'm under strict orders not to let the patient speak to anyone until he's been questioned by the top brass. So, if you're satisfied Mr. Brady has recovered from his ordeal it's time to—"

At that moment, a white coated doctor, clipboard in hand, pushed through the door of the room and strode briskly toward Scott's bed. I blinked. Did a double-take.

Ben?

"And how is our patient feeling this morning?" he boomed.

"Amazing," snarled Scott. "You try vomiting for a six hour stretch and see how you feel."

Ben poked him none too gently in the chest with his clipboard. "If this young lady hadn't been close by yesterday you wouldn't be feeling anything now—you'd be dead."

Scott had the good grace to look apologetic. "Sorry. You're right. I'm not my usual cheerful self at the moment." He stretched one hand out to me. "Thank you."

I shook his hand and felt a slip of paper transfer from his hand to mine. I slipped it into my pocket.

"That's it. Definitely no touching," spluttered Officer Patterson, his face turning pink. "Your time's up, Ms. McKinley. I want you to leave."

"Excuse me, Officer," said Doctor Ben stepping between the policeman and me. "Is your face usually pink?"

The policeman blinked, then transferred his gaze to the doctor. "Pink?"

"Yes. Pink."

"Um…no. I don't think so."

"Hmm…" Ben peered more closely at the man's face. "You haven't been near our patient without wearing a mask have you?"

The policeman, eyes bugging, mouth slack, nodded.

"Oh dear. That means you may have inhaled deadly carbon monoxide." Ben, face grim, shook his head slowly from side to side. "That could cause all sorts of unpleasant side effects unless treated immediately."

"What do you mean? What…what sort of problems?"

"Oh, research is presently being conducted on the effects of carbon monoxide poisoning on rats. Let's see…labored breathing, dizziness, flu-like symptoms, spots on the tongue and oh yes…several male rats in the program have become impotent."

My mouth opened. Closed. Then shot open again.

Scott went a funny shade of green.

The young policeman grabbed at his essentials and went an identical color.

After sending me a surreptitious wink, Doctor Ben reached for his new patient's wrist. "Here, let me take your pulse, Officer—see if you're showing any signs of agitation."

My back to Doctor Ben and his patient, I perched on the side of Scott's bed. "I have two questions for you," I whispered to Scott. "Did you kill Jack Lantana? And where is my sister?"

One hand partly covering his mouth, Scott pretended to wipe at his lips. "No, to the first—and I'm not sure to the second. Kat, I *didn't* write that suicide note and *wasn't* trying to commit suicide. Some asshole must have drugged my drink at the track, 'cos when I woke up I was inhaling pure poison and was too weak to do shit-all about it."

"Good."

"*Good*? What part of my horrific experience do you define as good?"

"The part that says you're not the bad guy." I smiled at him. "If you were—it would mean Liz's choice in men was down there with her wacky lifestyle."

"Thank you. I think."

Before continuing, I glanced over my shoulder at Officer Patterson. The poor man was perched on the edge of a chair, tongue protruding, while Doctor Ben examined said appendage for little white spots. White spots—according to the sage doctorly advice being given—was a *very bad* sign.

"You said in your text that Liz was in trouble. What sort of trouble?"

"She overheard someone talking about how the slow dogs were winning races. Wouldn't tell me, but she planned to confront Bob Germaine, the acting-secretary of the greyhound club. I told her to go to the police, but she doesn't trust the cops. Said they'd laugh at her because the victims were only dogs. Anyway, when I rung Liz an hour later, her phone was switched off. That was Friday morning and I haven't been able to contact her since. I thought if I met you, told you about it, *you* could talk to Bob Germaine."

"Why didn't you talk to him yourself?"

"Tried to. He said I was delusional. Said he hadn't set eyes on my idiot girlfriend and ordered me off the track."

I could hear Officer Patterson becoming loud and stroppy behind me. Probably due to the fact that Ben had requested he drop his pants in readiness for a rectal examination.

"Scott," I said, leaning forward, "first you tell me Liz is missing from a rabbiter's hut and now you say she's missing after fronting the stand-in secretary of the local greyhound racing club. Which story is true? And how can I believe a word you say?"

Scott, suddenly looking exhausted, ran a hand across his forehead and leant back against the pillows. "Seems Liz met up with some guys protesting about mining in Arkaroola the first time and went off with them for a few days without letting me know."

"And the blood in the shack?"

"Cut her finger while making bamboo baskets for homeless dogs."

"So now you want me to—"

"Outside! Both of you!" Officer Patterson, face now a very unhealthy shade of puce stormed across to the bed and pointed a stiff finger at the door.

"Well, if you're sure—" Ben began.

"Sure? Sure?" Officer Patterson spluttered, dancing on the spot. For a moment I thought he was going to explode into thousands of messy pink pieces right there on the sterile gray hospital floor. "The only thing I'm sure of is that something fishy is going on here." He glared at Doctor Ben whose stethoscope dangled precariously from around his left ear. "What I'm *not* sure of is that you're a real doctor." He rested one hand on his gun and his glare intensified. "So, if this room isn't cleared of all but the patient by the time I count to five, I'll arrest you both, call for backup and you can prove your credentials down at the station."

I scrambled to my feet, Ben rescued his borrowed stethoscope before it hit the ground and by the time the irate policeman got to *three* we were gone.

20

My sister, Liz, was like the invisible woman. Here one minute—poof—gone the next. Had she merely bumped into a new group of protesters and marched off into the sunset, all primed to right another wrong? Or was there something more sinister to her second disappearance after talking to Bob Germaine?

As we drove from the hospital to Kenny Gilbert's place, I gazed out the car window at the water trickling along the gutters into drains, at the tarmac still wet from the storm of yesterday, and tried to compare a picture of the present Liz with the baby sister I'd grown up with and loved. Images of Liz at six with a bloodied nose after intervening when a bully twice her size had tied a tin can to the tail of one of the local cats. The bully had pulled her hair and punched her in the nose but although busy letting off a series of earsplitting screams, Liz had still managed to untie the can before the cat took off up the nearest tree. I sighed. Guess my little sister had always tried to right life's wrongs. And yes, I loved her but was no closer to finding her.

However, this time I had a lead.

"Drop me off at the track," I told Ben as we turned into the road which led past the Port Augusta Greyhound track. "While you collect your dogs from Kenny's, I'll have a chat with Bob Germaine. See what he can tell me about Liz's visit."

"Want me to come in with you?"

I tutted, rolled my eyes, and punched him lightly on the arm. "Ben, I'm a big girl. I can have a conversation with another man without you flexing your muscles in the background and putting the poor guy off his morning tea. Just go pick up your dogs. I'll meet you out the front of the track in half an hour. Okay?"

"And if you're not there I'll dress up in a sheriff's outfit and come galloping to the rescue."

"Hmm…you'd look sexy in a Stetson," I said.

"Just a Stetson?"

"Well…perhaps I'd let you wear your gun belt too."

"And my cowboy boots?"

"Okay, but that's the limit. Anything else and it would spoil the picture."

"What about spurs? Cowboy boots are no fun without spurs."

"Go!" I said waving him off with a laugh.

"Maybe tonight?" With a grin so hot it would leave old maids swooning and even centenarians reaching for their vibrators, he drove off, leaving me standing on the footpath outside the dog track.

Mind and body reacting to the image of a near-naked Ben with silver spurs fastened to his embossed cowboy boots, I closed my eyes. Gulped a cooling breath of fresh air. There'd be time for naked cowboy games later—like tonight. My mission at the moment was to grill a suspect without him realizing he was under suspicion. Before I barged in on Bob Germaine, I needed to prepare a suitable list of questions to ask him. Like what was his connection to the slow dog scam? Did he kill Jack Lantana and shove him in the fridge? Did he steal Stanley? Was he involved in Liz's disappearance and if so, where the hell had he hidden her?

All posed in a subtle manner topped with my inimitable PI charm— of course.

However, as I trekked across the car park, I was unable to stop myself from staring at the crime scene tape strung around the corner of the park. Scott had come very close to dying in that spot. I shivered and pulled my coat closer around my body. Was it a case of attempted suicide because of guilt—or attempted murder by an unknown villain?

The race track itself was empty, except for a grey-coated, track maintenance guy revving a noisy tractor on the far side of the raceway near the 400 metre starting boxes. Not bothering to check with him, I headed for a small brick building marked *Office*, pushed through the wooden glass fronted doorway and pinged the little silver bell at the front desk.

"Hello, anyone around?"

No office worker poked her head around the corner or jumped up from behind the copying machine. No cleaning lady came at me waving her mop or broom. No suspicious interim-secretary shot out of his cubby hole with a gun or dagger. Okay. So…what would Stephanie Plum do in this situation? Opt for a chance to search for clues in the empty office or beat a hasty retreat? Hmm. Probably choose the option that didn't involve the likelihood of being caught and charged with burglary, trespass and countless other criminal offenses. Although come to think of it, our favorite bounty hunter always had Ranger or Morelli to pull strings for her when she bombed out.

I smiled. Felt a tickle in my knickers. Why should I be envious? I had my semi-naked cowboy.

From my position in front of the enquiry counter, I could see a small room leading off the main office with SECRETARY etched on the glass door. The door was open. The room was empty. Undecided, I licked my lips and swayed from side to side. Maybe I could take just a tiny peek inside and if anyone found me, I could say I was waiting for Bob Germaine. Unless of course it was Bob himself who found me and I happened to be nose deep in one of his open desk drawers at the time.

Pushing that chilling thought aside as too stressful to waste time on, I slipped into the office and glanced around the room. What was I expecting to find? A pale pink writing pad in the middle of his desk showing a detailed map of where he'd stashed my sister? Geez…what was I even doing here? I didn't know for certain whether Liz had managed to query Germaine about the slow dogs. Maybe she'd been distracted and taken off with another group of professional protesters all steamed up about some hundred-year-old gum tree that needed saving. Maybe Germaine was telling the truth and Liz hadn't got around to seeing him. There again, maybe he was lying through his perfectly aligned, expensively-maintained teeth and he'd squirrelled my baby sister away in an unused shed on the track grounds because he was the mastermind behind the scam with the slow dogs. Or maybe I needed to go home and rest up, take a couple of Panadol Forte and calm down. After all, I had a team of racing dogs waiting for me, and Liz had looked after herself without my intervention since leaving home five years ago. Why start now? I gritted my teeth and intensified my search—because my little sister might be in trouble.

The papers on the desk seemed to be mainly racing nomination forms so after quickly flipping through them, I wriggled the flashing red mouse beside the computer until the screensaver disappeared. And did a double take. Oh boy! I grabbed a quick breath and closed my mouth with a snap. Three naked women lay entwined on a bed—and they sure weren't sleeping. I blinked and felt a headache coming on. Who'd have thought a camera could see that far up…

Bemused, I dragged my eyes from the graphic images and clicked on History. More explicit sites—plus similar breeding websites to the ones I found on Jack Lantana's computer. What was the significance of greyhound breeding websites displaying the names of racing dogs with their sire and dam and litter mates? Was it a curious coincidence that Bob and Jack shared the same interest in the breeding of racing dogs— or a hot clue? No time to figure that out now. I took a deep breath. Would Stephanie take out her a nail file and open the suspiciously locked top drawer of Bob Germaine's desk or would she examine the contents of his waste paper basket?

As I wasn't a nail file carrying sort of person, I upended the waste paper basket onto the floor and surveyed the contents. Screwed up papers, several unwanted brochures, a couple of empty McDonald's packets and a revolting piece of rubber that looked awfully like a used condom.

"Can I help you, Katrina?"

I froze. Surrounded by incriminating evidence, I grabbed a quick breath and slowly turned around ready to run if necessary.

Oh, God. Half-in, half-out of the doorway, virtually blocking my exit, stood the man I'd come to question, Bob Germaine. As usual, his smile displayed perfectly aligned teeth, but the coldness in those unnerving black eyes reminded me of a snake eying off the tasty live mouse he'd selected for breakfast.

He raised his bushy eye brows. "Tell me, Katrina, is examining other people's rubbish a bizarre idiosyncrasy of yours—or are you looking for something in particular?"

"Bob?" Even my voice sounded like a squeaky mouse ready to bolt for the nearest mouse-hole. Except the only hole big enough for me to dart through was the doorway and the big bad snake had claimed that one.

"Katrina?"

"Um…" I stared down at the polished wooden floor where a dollop of ketchup had leaked from the remains of a Big Mac packet and left an ugly red stain that could have easily passed for blood. I closed my eyes and asked the Universe for a perfectly good reason to be standing beside this man's desk surrounded by his detritus. "Well, you know me, Bob," I said with a self-derogatory shrug, still panning the Universe. "I've always been a bit of a klutz. What happened—I was waiting to see you and-and—somehow tripped over the waste paper basket, and tipped it over." *Phew!* I got down on my knees and reached for a mangy half-chewed biscuit that had skittered under his desk. "Don't worry though, I'll pick it all up."

All except that revolting rubber thing…

Bob Germaine moved three steps closer. I knew it was three steps because with each stride his shiny black loafers slapped against the wooden floor and sent vibrations skittering up through my knees.

"And to what do I owe the pleasure of this visit, Katrina?" His voice mocked me and I didn't need to look up to feel his eyes boring through the top of my head. "If it's photo-copying or a nomination query, you're too late. My staff went home earlier, as soon as the Sunday morning trials finished. In fact, there's no-one here but me." He paused and the air chilled several more degrees. "Even old McKenzie out there has finished grading the track and gone home to lunch."

On my knees I stared up at the man I thought I knew. He'd been a fellow greyhound trainer before giving up to work as a temp on the Greyhound Control Board. From my vantage point on the floor, Bob Germaine appeared seven feet tall and although his smile didn't shift, the stillness of his mouth made him even more menacing. Butterflies staggered around in my stomach like a mob of drunks. This man may be a killer and I was alone with him. Damn! Why the heck didn't I let Ben come with me when he offered? My cowboy wasn't due for at least another fifteen minutes and by that time my chopped up body could be packed and stored in the canteen's refrigerator.

I stumbled to me feet, dropped the half-eaten biscuit into the bin and wiped my hands on the seat of my jeans. Oh well, if I was going to be murdered I wanted some questions answered first. "Bob, what did my sister tell you when she came to see you on Friday?"

His smile slipped and confusion clouded his eyes. "Your sister? I didn't know you had a sister, Katrina. I thought you were checking out what I watch on my computer."

"Bob, I couldn't care less if your eyeballs exploded from watching threesomes perform in bed. I'm here about my sister. Her name is Liz. A hippy type. I believe she tried to give you information she'd overheard about how slow dogs were winning on country tracks."

"That's your *sister*?" His look was almost sympathetic. "That ditzy dame that causes trouble everywhere she goes?"

Yep. Sounded like Liz. I nodded.

He dragged a hand through his hair without disturbing one immaculate strand. Amazing. Must be gelled to within an inch of its life. "Look," he said, "I've already told that other troublemaker, Scott Brady, I haven't seen his pesky girlfriend since she tagged along with him and tried to create chaos, claiming we were racing greyhounds against their will—which is when I told her if she stepped on the track again I'd ring the police and have her charged with trespass and causing a disturbance. So… I'm sorry, but if your rabble-rousing sister *has* disappeared, I say, good riddance."

"But she came to see you on Friday." I crossed my fingers behind my back. "I have proof."

His smile vanished which was good because the perpetual sight of those whiter-than-white shark teeth was doing my head in. "What do you mean…you have proof? Who told you that fruitcake came here?" His snake eyes turned into sharp pebbles. "You can't prove a thing. It's their word against mine."

Aha. So I was right. Liz *did* talk to Bob Germaine about what she'd overhead regarding the slow dogs winning. Thing is—after their conversation, did Liz walk away from his office and then take off with another bunch of professional protesters—or did Bob Germaine make sure she couldn't walk anywhere again?

He stepped closer. So close, I could see the ring of sweat forming under his armpits and smell the strong odor of his musky aftershave. "And what if she did come in here with some cock-and-bull story about how there was a betting scam going on?" he growled. "I told her what I'm telling you—keep your nose out of what doesn't concern you. Long priced dogs pop up every day of the week, from here to Timbuktu. It's the fickleness of the game. As long as the winning dog's swab comes back negative, it's all above board."

"But—"

"Now, if you've finished sifting through my trash and checking out my computer—I think you'd better go."

"How much money did *you* win on the slow dog that won today, Bob?"

"I said, you've outstayed your welcome."

"Are you in league with the scammers, Bob?"

"Are you deaf—or just as thick as your idiot sister?"

"Does that mean you know where my sister is?"

"I have nothing more to say to you, Katrina." His anger almost palpable, Bob's mouth twisted and his face, now coated in sweat, came close to touching mine. I cringed away from the sweat and the barely controlled rage, both hands cradling my stomach where butterflies lurched into the air, crashing and bouncing off the walls. "So, do I have to pick you up and throw you out—or are you going to leave on your own two feet?"

There was a shuffling movement near the door and the distinct sound of jingling spurs. "Am I in time for morning tea? If so, I'll have a strong black with three lumps, please." Ben swaggered into the room, a borrowed Stetson jammed hard on his head. "And unless you'd rather those lumps were beaten into your head with my fist, Germaine—I'd move away from my girlfriend. Right now."

21

Fɪꜰᴛᴇᴇɴ ᴍɪɴᴜᴛᴇꜱ ʟᴀᴛᴇʀ, Ben drove through the township of Port Augusta and out onto the main highway back to Adelaide. Smiling, I relaxed into the passenger seat. No doubt about it, Benjamin Taylor was handy to have around in a tight fix. Even when we were just good mates, in the days before Ben recognized my womanly assets, he'd always been there for me. Now, however, there was an added dimension to his protectiveness.

Could it possibly be love?

Okay, when my urban cowboy came bursting through the doorway to my rescue, he didn't actually toss me over the pommel of his saddle and gallop off into the sunset—neither did he leave the bad guy flat on his back, battered and bruised and with his butt well and truly kicked— but his timely entrance certainly changed the dynamics in the room. Immediately Bob Germaine's ugly threats dissolved into cowardly whines. He didn't even protest when Ben expressed his opinion that a man who felt the need to become physical and threaten a woman was either insecure—or had been inflicted with a puny underdeveloped penis that he couldn't get up.

It was a long drive home. With a trailer load of dogs hooked on behind the car we probably had three hours driving ahead of us. What's worse—it had started to rain again. I shivered under my jacket and peered through the car window. This was serious rain. Large bloated drops that sent our windscreen wipers into a frenzy of activity. Overhead, the sky hung like a thick dark curtain and although the middle of the day, Ben switched on the car's headlights. Leaning forward, I bumped the heater up a notch then settled back in my seat to mull things over in my head.

Okay, what had I really learned from questioning Bob Germaine? Not much. Perhaps I was wrong about him. Perhaps the man's temper tantrum was more to do with me poking my nose into his computer's hard drive and discovering his less-than-moral taste in downloads than any involvement in the slow dog scam or my sister's disappearance.

Ben shifted in the seat beside me. "You *do* realize you need to work on your interview techniques, don't you?"

Huh? Mouth open, I stared at him. Was my boyfriend psychic? Did he just read my mind?

I narrowed my eyes in his direction and gave a warning sniff. Nah. He was having a go at me. "What do you mean, *Benjamin*?"

Dark eyes dancing wickedly, Ben shot me a quick grin. "Hey…don't bite my head off, babe. I'm only basing my opinion on the color of Bob Germaine's face when I interrupted your interview back there." He cocked his head to one side, frowned and pretended to deliberate the issue. "And of course your victim's parting words to me—'control your girlfriend—keep her on a leash—she's a menace to society'."

"Bob Germaine is not a *victim*—he's a *suspect*."

"Riiight."

"And his face was red from temper."

"So your interviewing technique didn't have anything to do with making him spit the dummy?"

I wriggled in my seat. "Yeah, but—"

"Remember Katrina, I was also with you the day you grilled Big Mick, our dodgy bookmaker friend, at his house. Mick's face then was exactly the same shade of puce as Bob's today."

I scowled at the passing scenery. Other than spinifex grass, prickle bushes and the occasional stunted tree, the never-ending land stretched flat and brown and wet on both sides of the bitumen roadway.

"Excuse me for breathing," I growled, "but all I did was what any other concerned citizen would do in the same situation."

"Which is?"

"I asked Bob Germaine if he had anything to do with Liz's disappearance or the slow dog scam."

A smile twitched at the corners of Ben's lips. "Right. And I suppose you were subtle, delicate, restrained, and the ultimate professional in your approach? In other words you didn't blast him with these questions straight out? Didn't indicate in any way shape or form that you thought he was up to his eyeballs in skullduggery?"

"Well…"

"I rest my case."

Damn. Maybe I did need to brush up on my PI techniques. Maybe I should watch more CSI on TV, read more mysteries and study how Jessica Fletcher, Kinsey Millhone and Nancy Drew approached the art of interrogation. I blew out a sigh of frustration. *Subtle?* Okay, but whenever *I* attempted *subtle*, I didn't get a direct answer—more like an eye roll.

I blew out another sigh and relaxed my muscles, one by one. Strung out as I was from questioning Scott at the hospital and then the ill-tempered Bob Germaine, I was surprised to find my eye lids growing heavy. The regular drone of the rain on the roof of the car and the swish of wheels on wet bitumen acted like a lullaby and next I knew Ben was shaking my shoulder.

"Come on Sleeping Beauty, wake up. We're home."

"Whaaat?" I said and blinked owl-like at the familiar surroundings outside the car window. My graveled driveway—my chocolate box, two-storied house—the sound of excited barking not only from behind my welcoming front door but from the kennel house at the end of the path.

Ben helped me undo my seatbelt and then stood back and watched as I scrambled out of the car and stretched. "Next time we travel together," he said, straight-faced, "remind me to store a few clothes pegs in the glove box. You snored like an express train all the way home."

Dodging my hook to the kidneys, he laughed and dropped a quick kiss on my forehead. "See you tonight, gorgeous. Can't stop, 'cos I gotta get my dogs home. They'll be itching to get out of the trailer and stretch their legs."

"After that clothes peg quip, you'd better bring chocolates if you want to see me tonight, Benjamin. And only the biggest, most expensive box in the shop will do."

The strident ring of the phone greeted me as I pushed past my two bouncing dogs and stumbled into the lounge room. Geez. Anyone would think I'd been away for a year instead of a day. While dishing out pats and cuddles and exchanging kisses with my welcoming committee, I lifted the hands free from its base and pressed TALK.

"Kat McKinley."

"Hey, Kat." It was Dr. Terry Chapman, the vet. "Any luck locating Stanley?"

"No…nothing yet."

"Don't worry, we'll find him." Terry's voice, as always, brimmed with confidence. "I've contacted the animal rescue services and left the dog's description at every vet surgery in South Australia. Someone, somewhere, will find your dog and when they do they'll bring him in." There was a short pause. "Talking about Stanley, there was something else I wanted to discuss with you."

I plopped down onto the lounge, lifted the wriggling Tater into my lap and tossed Lucky's favorite squeaky purple dragon across the room for her to fetch. "Go on. I'm all ears."

"Due to the confusion at the surgery on Friday, I didn't get around to explaining what I discovered when I examined Stanley prior to neutering."

"Confusion? Geez more like World War Three erupting," I said scratching the special spot behind Tater's ear. As usual, it made him purr like a cat. "Come to think of it I *do* remember you mentioning something about Stanley's ear brands—but that's around the time the poor squashed cat and the legless bird were brought into the surgery and I discovered Stanley was missing."

"Well, when I checked Stanley, I noticed the ear brand on one ear was difficult to read. Of course this happens often which is why micro-chipping is gradually taking the place of ear branding. Anyway, after studying the ear more closely under a microscope I wrote the numbers down. Got a pen handy?"

I yanked at the front drawer of the coffee table and rummaged around until I found a small notebook and a biro. "Yep. Go ahead."

"His right ear brand is S418. Okay? Now, it might pay to check this against Stanley's racing papers because what's suspicious is the fact that the last number has been changed from a 6 to an 8."

Perplexed, I stared at the numbers I'd scribbled on the first page of the notebook. Who would change the dog's ear brand? And why? Was Purple Pants, the man we'd found in the refrigerator, responsible for this? Or was it his killer?

"Another thing," went on Terry—as if this wasn't enough to comprehend already. "Did you know Stanley has a white sock on his left front leg?"

"No."

"You can't see it because someone has covered the sock with a dark colored dye."

I stared at the phone. As Alice remarked when confronted by the weird goings on in Wonderland—*this was getting curiouser and curiouser.*

"Plus," continued Terry, "the white toenails on the same foot have also been dyed." He paused again and I imagined him running his fingers through his thick hair which is what Terry always did when overexcited. "So…it looks like our dearly beloved GAP dog is actually part of the mystery."

I frowned. "So it wasn't Lofty they were after at all?"

"Nope."

"It was Stanley all the time—and now they have him."

"Unfortunately."

"Guess I'll have to start calling you Sherlock."

Terry let out a chuckle. "Nah. That Sherlock guy was a wimpy drama queen—left all the work to his side-kick, Dr. Watson. Me—I'd rather be Perry Mason. You know, a day in court to demonstrate the brilliance of my mind, followed by cocktails in a nightclub at five."

I stood up and began to pace—much to the disgust of Tater who slid off my lap onto the lounge with a disgruntled growl. "Okay, Perry Mason, after all that, I think it's time we bumped up the search for Stanley. I have a shaky feeling he's in more trouble than we bargained for."

"You're right. I have to attend to my next patient right now, but after that I'll get onto my contacts, see if they've heard anything. There's something strange going on here."

I placed the handset back on the base and scooped Tater up in my arms. There was something strange going on alright and I had a feeling Terry's discovery was a major clue to the secret of the slow dog saga.

Were faster litter mates being used as *ring-ins* and entered in races under the name of their slower relatives?

22

"Ben should've tied Germaine's nose in knots and shoved the whole freaking mess down his throat." Tanya's rant indicted if she'd been with me at the time, another of Germaine's appendages would have copped a similar serve.

It was four hours later—close to 7 pm. The rain had stopped but a strong gusty wind rattled the loose window in the laundry. The one I meant to get fixed and only remembered on windy nights when tradesmen were tucked up at home, downing a couple of pints and fixing their own loose windows. After working and feeding my racing team, I'd settled them down for the night and given my best friend a ring.

Of course the phone call lasted all of two minutes. *What the blue-blazes!*, had been Tanya's immediate reaction when I told her about someone trying to kill Scott and then she'd promptly invited herself over for dinner and was standing at my front door with two enormous steaks—before I could even warm up the grill.

Ben wasn't coming for dinner. He'd rung to tell me Pot O' Gold, his favorite brood bitch, had decided to go into labor five days early, and nothing short of an earthquake would shift him from Goldie's side until every squirming puppy was safely lined up against the warm milk bar.

It was Erin's turn to stay with her father this week—so it was just Tanya and me. And that suited us fine.

Our steaks sizzled under the grill, the tantalizing smell sending my stomach into spasms and rumbles of anticipation. While I filled Tanya in on my Port Augusta adventures, I also sorted through dirty clothes ready to bundle in the washing machine. It's a fact of life that even when there's a killer on the loose and everything around you gets hectic and scary you still need clean clothes.

"Ben didn't *need* to get physical," I told Tanya. "It was enough to hear his spurs jingling as he pushed through the door and ordered Germaine to move away from his girl-friend. You know—in that no-nonsense, bone-melting voice of his that makes me almost wet my pants just thinking about ripping his clothes off and—"

"La, la, la…" Tanya covered her ears with both hands and shook her head. "Just get on with it, will ya?"

I laughed. Tanya's little black book was legendary, yet she balked at descriptions of what Ben and I got up to under the sheets…or on the floor…or in the cupboard…or…

"Okay. Okay. Anyway, one minute Germaine was throwing a temper tantrum complete with red face and flying spittle and the next he was quaking in his three hundred dollar shiny black loafers and backing right away from me."

"Typical, chicken-shit bully!" Tanya, who had the job of going through pockets in search of hidden tissues, hurled a pair of my black trackie pants into the washing machine as though she was hurling Germaine off a cliff. "All piss and no wind."

I grinned. My trusty sidekick oozed self-confidence…and bad axioms. With her at my side, I was sure we could devise a brilliant Plan A—plus several backup plans in case Plan A wasn't so brilliant after all and slammed us nose first into the nearest brick wall.

I yanked my jumper over my head and tossed it in the machine. Green dribble, courtesy of Lucky, decorated the front. "Germaine's definitely up to something crooked, but whether he's worried about the porn I found on his computer or involved in the slow dog scam or he really does know where Liz's gone—it's anybody's guess." I lifted one eyebrow and focused on my cock-sparrow friend. "Thing is, Tan, we need a plan."

She hesitated. "We do?"

Surely that wasn't a squeak? A crack forming in Supergirl's sexy amour? "How else are we going to find Liz and the dogs involved in the scam?"

"You're right." She bent to pick up a pair of my jeans from the clothes on the floor of the laundry, slid her hand into the back pocket. "Er…don't suppose you got a beer in your fridge?"

Oh! Uh! We weren't going down *that* path again. "Tan, the only drinks you'll find in my fridge have too many calories and too much caffeine but *no* alcohol content."

"Spoilsport," she growled. "You're no fun at—hey, what's this?"

I glanced up from a tug of war with Lucky, who'd claimed one of my thick purple socks, to see Tanya holding a small folded piece of colored paper between two fingers.

After tossing my jeans into the washing machine she unfolded the paper, read the print, and frowned. "This was in the back pocket of your jeans."

"And?"

"It's Gina Robertson's address." Her frown deepened. "And it's been torn off a GAP brochure."

And then it hit me. "*Of course!* Scott snuck that to me when I visited him in the hospital. I slipped it into my back pocket—and with all that happened afterwards—forgot about it."

"But why would Scott give you Gina's address? What's Lady Muck got to do with anything? And surely he'd realize you knew where our Goody-Two-Shoes GAP co-coordinator lived. And anyway, why would you *want* to know?"

I was as confused as Tanya and when she passed me the scrap of paper, I turned it upside down and then checked out the back—nothing there—except Gina's address. "Got me stumped," I said and my head spun with unanswered questions. "In the hospital we had this officious rent-a-cop breathing over our shoulders, refusing to let us discuss the case. I remember asking Scott if his girlfriend had been in to see him—meaning Liz—and that's when he pretended to thank me for saving his life. He shook my hand and palmed that piece of paper to me." I stared at Tanya. "Does this mean Scott thinks Liz is at Gina's place?"

"But why would your sister go to Gina's? Doesn't make sense."

I closed my eyes for a moment, trying to calm my bongo-drum heartbeat. "Unless Liz had no say in the matter."

"You mean—"

"What if Liz was kidnapped because she knew too much about the slow dog scam."

"And she's been locked up somewhere on Gina's property." Tanya's fists clenched and her top lip curled. "Which *also* means our sainted GAP coordinator is in this up to her long pointed nose."

"Hard to believe."

"Well, why else would Liz's boyfriend palm you that piece of paper?"

I shrugged. Like all the other questions, I had no answer to that one. "Thing is, Tan, what are we going to do about it?"

"Well…" Tanya, the corners of her mouth tweaking, sent me a wicked wink. "We *could* go over and beat the truth out of her. Blacken her eyes, break both arms, string her up on the wall and poke sharp sticks in her eyes."

"Yeah, that'd be fun," I agreed, joining in the fantasy. "After that, we could tie her to the back of our car and drag her across a few miles of rough, stony, bush land."

"Then," continued Tanya, with an evil laugh that would have done Freddy Kruger proud. "If she *still* won't divulge her secrets—we could always employ that ex-boyfriend of hers, Cory Palmer. You know, The Chronic Whinger. Hell, we'd only need to let him loose on her for a couple of hours and she'd be begging to give us information—just to stop him whining."

The thought of Liz locked up somewhere, scared and confused and maybe hurt, brought me back from whimsy to stark reality.

"Or…" I said, switching on the washing machine and leading the way into the kitchen, "we could just keep an eye on whoever goes in and out of Gina's place during the day and then, as soon as it's dark, break into the property and take a look through her sheds. See if we can find either the dogs involved in the scam—or my elusive sister."

"Well…it so happens, my Scrooge-of-a-boss, who was feeling magnanimous due to a rise in profits for the year, has given me a rare flexi morning off tomorrow," said Tanya lifting the already prepared salad bowl from the fridge and placing it in the middle of the table next to the pepper and salt and tomato sauce. "So…while you're busy training your dogs, I can do the first shift and you can take over in the afternoon while I go to work."

She rubbed her hands together and drooled as I set one textbook-cooked steak on each plate together with a pile of caramelized onions.

"Good," I said as we scraped our chairs up to the table and grabbed our knives and forks like weapons of war. "Then tomorrow night we carry out—*Operation Find Liz.*"

The first bite of tender, slowly grilled fillet steak, medium cooked, dripping juices and oozing flavor, spread like warm honey into every crevice of my taste buds as I chewed.

And all conversation promptly stopped.

23

I SAT STRAIGHT UP IN BED. Instantly awake.

What—or who—had set every one of the sixteen dogs outside in the kennel house barking?

I tried to take a deep breath—but between my heart hammering high in my throat, and the room, blacker than the inside of a killer's mind—breathing didn't come easily.

I turned my head toward the night-stand beside my bed. The numbers, glowing red on the digital alarm clock, told me it was 1am. Three hours since Tanya had gone home.

Why were the dogs barking?

I shivered and resisted the urge to pull the duvet over my head and pretend deafness. Perhaps if I let the dogs bark long enough someone would come over from next door and investigate the noise—and find my mutilated body cut up in a hundred bloody pieces and spoiling the sheets—all because I'd been too chicken to get out of bed?

Oh, God, don't go there...

Stretched out across my feet, Lucky emitted a sleepy snuffle and turned over on her other side. Some guard dog. Not so Tater—hackles bristling, a warning growl deep in his tiny throat, he was on full alert and waiting for my order to: *Attack! Kill! Destroy!*

My hand resting on his head, I felt warmth creep into my chilled bones and spread into my chicken heart. If a dog weighing no more than half pound of butter could be fearless under fire—so could I.

"It's probably only that ugly feral cat again," I told my miniature stegosaurus, who agreed and promised to eat the cat in the morning—after he'd licked up his corn flakes.

Feeling braver, I tumbled out of bed, switched on the light and reached for my dressing gown.

Not that I planned to personally investigate whatever had set the dogs off. Oh no, no, no. I'd been cured of doing idiotic things in the middle of the night after being hit on the head by a man who I thought was my friend. My erstwhile client, Peter Manning, who thankfully was now spending the next twenty or thirty years at his Majesty's pleasure.

With Tater hot on my heels, I pattered barefoot down the stairs to the landing and pressed a specially installed dog-switch, high on the wall. Although I couldn't hear the result from inside the house, I knew a soothing classical CD would now be working its magic in the dog kennels. This week's musical selection was Brahms. Hungarian dance music followed by the hauntingly beautiful 'Wiegenlied, Op. 49, No 4'—better known to us mere mortals as 'Brahms's Lullaby'. So I knew it wouldn't be long before the barking subsided to an occasional sleepy yap.

Tater and I were now wide awake and heading for the kitchen. "Yep! Definitely that feral cat," I said, more to reassure myself than the dog. "Now, how about a hot chocolate for me and a bowl of warm milk for you?"

My trusty sidekick thought that would go down nicely, thank you very much.

Ten minutes later, with Tater snuggled up on my lap and fingers wrapped around a half-empty mug of hot chocolate topped with marshmallows, I lay my head back on the lounge chair and puffed out a sigh. Stanley's altered ear brand niggled at me. He must have been the fast dog in his litter selected as a *ring-in* for a slower litter mate. But where was Stanley and his slower brother now? Were they even still alive? And what about the dog who raced and won at huge odds at Port Augusta yesterday? It wasn't *Go Rambo*—it was one of his faster litter mates. The real Rambo couldn't beat a two-legged centipede to the water bucket and back—even on a 40 degree day. No wonder the fake Rambo didn't know me. And on reflection, there'd been something different about the dog's ears. The genuine Rambo's ears were longer, pointier, whereas his substitute's ears were smaller and flatter.

If only I knew what the perpetrators of the scam did with the greyhounds after they'd raced? And then another thought crossed my mind. Maybe if I found the dogs' secret hiding place—I'd find Liz and her team of protesters looking after them.

Craaaaaaash!

I froze. My heart, threatening cardiac arrest, stopped beating for at least 30 seconds before it burst into wild erratic flight again.

"Holy crap!" I lurched from the chair. Hot chocolate spewed in an arc. Tater erupted off my lap, his high pitched bark threatening to tear apart whoever or whatever lay on the other side of the front door.

Me? I couldn't stop shaking. Where the hell was my alter-ego, *Bombshell Chick,* when I needed her? Evidently out getting her hair frosted. Finger nails half way down my throat, legs weaker than Grandma McKinley's morning cup of tea, I inched across the room into the passageway and stood, holding my breath, ears on stalks, listening. Was someone on the other side of the front door waiting to do me in, or had they merely tried to scare me to death, and then left? I tiptoed toward the door—not to open it—hell, no—but to switch on the outside light and peer through the eye-hole.

By this time the greyhounds in the kennel house were barking again and Lucky had trotted down the stairs, a purple dinosaur dangling from her mouth. Not sure whether to growl or wag her tail in case we had a visitor, Lucky stood staring at the front door, pieces of purple felt peeping from around her teeth. Not so Tater. Tiny feet dancing on the spot, hair on the back of his neck standing up like pins on a pin cushion, he was geared up ready to chew on whoever's ankles happened to walk through that door.

Eyes squinting, I leant against the door and scanned the limited view through the security hole. The light from the outside globe shone on the front verandah and then spread out like hot butter onto the driveway. But no-one was there. No alien monsters. No killers. Not even a noisy ghost. And the only movement I could see came from the wind bending a group of rose bushes at the top of the driveway.

I had to see more…

Hands inexplicably growing an extra set of thumbs, I fumbled to unlock the door, left the chain on the hook, and stuck my nose through the three inch opening. From the bottom of the door—a muddy red brick stared up at me. Okay. I could deal with that. I grabbed a quick breath and let it out slowly. One Oodnadatta. Two Oodnadatta. Three Oodnadatta…

Okay, I now had the solution to *what* had caused the crash—but not the *who*.

Did I really want to know the answer to that question?

Hell, no—but if I was going to get any more sleep tonight—

Ordering Tater to stay, I unhooked the latch, sent a message to the Universe to help find my elusive *Bombshell Chick,* and stepped outside the door.

And that's when my poor battered heart went crashing downhill tumbling over and over until it splattered against the rocks.

For across my front door—in splashes of red—wet paint still dribbling from the letters, like blood—were the words that caused my heart's demise.

YOU'RE NEXT!

24

This had to be a bad dream. Perhaps if I closed my eyes and counted to ten, it would go away. I opened my eyes. The nightmare was still there—in words a foot high—in words spray painted on the thick wooden varnish that sent fear, like a terminal disease, racing insidiously through my intestines.

Who'd left that message? Was it a threat or a promise? Was the spray-painter still lurking in the darkness, watching me, feeding off my fear?

It took me three goes before I finally convinced my feet to move. For me to spill inside the house, close the door and fumble the lock into place.

There'd be no more sleep for me tonight—in fact, I'd be lucky to ever sleep again. Words from Hamlet's famous soliloquy danced in my head.

'to die, to sleep no more'.

Fear clutched at my gut, twisted its grip a little tighter. I tried to clear the knot in my throat as I keyed in DI Adam's phone number but when he answered, the only word I could get out was…

Help!

*****

Detective Inspector Garry Adams, his five o'clock shadow more like a ten o'clock forest, sprawled on one of my kitchen chairs, legs stretched out in front of him. The wall clock, hands shaped like racing greyhounds, ticked off a minute's silence before revealing the time: 1.45 am. During the silence, the DI's dark eyes teased at me like a persistent fly. He then bent over his notebook and scribbled on the half-filled page before looking up with a pronounced sigh. "You ignored my advice, didn't you?"

"Advice?" I echoed, not sure which of the many lectures he'd given me he was referring to this time.

"I distinctly told you to leave catching criminals to the police."

"Oh. That advice."

"Let me put this another way, Ms. McKinley. Do you have any idea who would have reason to deface your front door?"

"Deface? Funny term for a death threat."

"It's not necessarily a death threat. 'You're next' could mean…many things."

"Like what?" I growled. "Like someone snuck onto my property in the dead of night to paint a message on my door in blood red paint—and throw a brick for good measure—just to remind me I'm next in line to see the doctor?" I yanked the thick plaid blanket the Inspector had taken off my sofa more firmly around my shoulders. "Not likely."

The familiar smell of dog clung to the rough blanket, comforting me. But the warmth couldn't stop me shivering. Someone out there was determined to scare me—or worse.

Adams swiveled his head in the direction of his assistant, the vinegary Constable Belinda Chalmers, who stood smirking in the background. I could almost read the thought bubble hovering over the woman's head: *stupid ditz deserves everything she gets*. "Ms. McKinley is suffering from shock," the Inspector informed her. "So stir yourself, Constable, and make a nice hot cup of coffee."

Chalmers' mouth gaped. Lucky for her, I'd doused the kitchen with fly spray the night before. "*Me?*" she squeaked. "You want *me* to make that woman coffee?" If looks were finely honed axes, I figured DI Adams's would now be trolling on the ground, hunting for his decapitated head.

However, Adams didn't appear to notice the incredulous snort or the tight lips or the rest of her pissed off body language. Instead, his hand moved to pat Lucky the greyhound, who was leaning up against his leg, adoring eyes smiling up at him. Tater, due to the fact that he was obsessed with raping Chalmers' ankles whenever he saw her, was locked in my bedroom.

When her superior didn't respond, the policewoman snatched the electric jug from the kitchen bench, filled it with water from the Pura tap over the sink and stabbed the three pronged plug in the direction of an electrical socket on the wall.

"Milk and two sugars for me, thanks," I said, enjoying the entertainment.

Her reply was a snort and I winced when another cupboard door slammed shut. At this rate I'd be renewing the hinges on all my kitchen cupboards before the end of the day.

"You know," DI Adams said flipping over a page of his dog-eared notebook while chewing on the end of his biro. "Over the past three months, we've had a gang of graffiti artists leaving their tags all over the neighborhood. They've been driving the residents insane with their spray paint. I wouldn't be surprised if—"

"If that's a graffiti tag on my front door, I'm the Queen of the Undead."

"Uh…huh," he muttered and I was left wondering whether he thought the royal title suited me or not. Then, with a determined shove upwards, he lumbered to his feet and approached the coffee making constable who was still banging cupboard doors. If she ground her teeth any harder we'd be whisking her off to an all-night dental clinic.

The DI stretched up and lifted an unopened jar of Nescafe down from a top shelf in my cupboard. "This what you're looking for Constable Chalmers?"

"Mmmgh."

The corners of his lips twitched as he added another Simpsons' mug to the one already on the bench. "Make that coffee for two, Constable."

He raised an eyebrow at me. "You don't mind if I join you, do you, Ms. McKinley?"

I shrugged. "Be my guest." And then I smiled up at Constable Chalmers. "You'll find chocolate biscuits in the larder, Constable. Bottom shelf. Behind the Coco-Pops."

DI Adams selected a teaspoon from the cutlery drawer and placed it in one of the mugs before making his way back to the table. For a man who'd only been in my kitchen a handful of times the Inspector seemed rather at home. Although, on reflection, I realized this gnarly policeman had been inside my house more times than my own mother…which was scary.

Before continuing our conversation, he carefully re-arranged his serge covered backside on the seat of the chair and encouraged Lucky to resume her leaning position against his leg. "Although I'm not saying you shouldn't be careful," he warned. "I don't want you jumping to conclusions and fearing the worst, either. This could merely be the act of a couple of half-witted kids playing out some crime show they've viewed on the idiot box."

"Or not." I added and then decided to change the subject. "By the way, did your policeman mates up North fill you in on what happened to Scott Brady? How he was the victim of an attempted murder?"

"You mean, suicide attempt. Yes, Senior Constable Mark Kelly contacted me yesterday. An interesting case. He also told me about your brave—or maybe some people would call foolhardy—reaction to the event."

"It wasn't suicide," I growled. "Someone slipped a drug into Scott's drink while he was at the track and he woke up inside his car with the gas full on."

"And you think the message on your front door—you're next—is from the same *someone*?"

"Could be."

Adams let out an exaggerated sigh before accepting a mug of coffee from Constable Chalmers. "I warned you, McKinley. I told you there are people out there who get a thrill from hurting others. But no, you wouldn't listen to me. You had to bulldoze your way in without a thought in your head and tread on toes that didn't relish being trodden on." He raised both caterpillar thick eyebrows at me and when I didn't comment, took a long slurp of his coffee. I was still waiting for mine. Probably still be waiting the day of my funeral—which the way things were looking could be sooner rather than later. "So, is there anything you want to tell me?" he persisted. "Anyone other than *me* you've ticked off lately?"

Let's see…

There was the owner of the grocery shop where I'd tripped and accidentally broke most of the free range eggs in his store display. There was the grumpy sports car driver who shook his fist at me when I cut him off and pinched his parking spot—only because I desperately needed to use the loo at the shopping center. Oh yeah and the tall scruffy guy who I'd first seen in Gina's barn and then at the track handling the Rambo look-alike. And of course the temporary racing-secretary who enjoyed watching threesomes and was prone to throwing temper tantrums…

I shook my head.

Not content to leave it there, Adams hung on like a dog with a bone. "Okay. Anything out of the ordinary you've poked your nose into lately that might have brought this on?"

Should I mention the scam? But what evidence did I have? An altered ear brand on a GAP dog and a slow greyhound I once trained coming in at 50/1? Hardly enough to prove my theory that the killer was also behind a *ring-in* scam. And of course this would set DI Adams off on another lecture about interfering in police business. I sighed. "You mean, other than looking for my sister because you lot don't seem to care?"

He drained his mug and set it back on the table. "Your sister wasn't actually missing at the time, Ms. McKinley. She was camped out with a mob of protesters whose main grievance seemed to be mining in

Arkaroola. And like the other protesters, your sister was doing her best to hinder the workmen and cause them to lose three days' pay."

"But she's gone missing again since then."

Adams gave a low exasperated groan which caused Lucky, still leaning against his leg, to nuzzle his crotch in sympathy. The DI brought out a crumpled carton of Dunhills from inside his coat pocket, extracted one virgin cigarette, stroked its length with the sensitivity of a man caressing a lover's face, lifted the cigarette to his nose and inhaled. I could see the tension rolling off his face as he spoke. "Is that so?"

"The last time anyone saw or heard from Liz was when she spoke to Bob Germaine on Friday. Don't you think that's odd?"

"Anything to do with your sister I consider odd, Ms. McKinley." He slid the cigarette gently back into the carton, returned the packet to his coat pocket and stood up. His frown seemed to suggest I'd spoiled a sensual sexual experience.

When his pager beeped, he snapped out a gruff, 'Adams here,' then listened, his frown deepening. "Right. I'm on my way." Then he turned to me. "A drive-by shooting has occurred at Munno Para so I have to go. But, don't worry, I've posted two constables on guard duty outside your house for the remainder of the night."

He looked at me and his frown softened. "But if you need me at all— I'm only a phone call away. Right?"

I nodded.

"Make sure all your doors and windows are locked when I leave. And open to no-one. I repeat—no-one. Is that clear?"

I nodded again. He really didn't need to tell me twice.

25

I WAS BENT DOUBLE, one arm hooked around Lofty's neck and wrestling the dog's left front leg into a bucket of iced water, when Tanya's text came through. With Lofty's aversion to water of any sort—hot or cold—I was too busy to check it out. However, after finally talking the *dog* into having his jarred wrist treated, I set the ultrasonic machine on pulse and juggled the mobile from my back pocket.

I'm bored. Zero happening here.

For a moment Tanya's message threw me. Then reality flooded in. Damn. What with the scare from the night before, I'd forgotten our plan to watch Gina's house today.

A 1 am visit from a killer tends to do that.

Mind elsewhere, I drew small underwater circles with the head of the ultrasonic machine on and around the greyhound's left wrist. Should I advise Tanya to go home and forget our plan? Let her know I was officially off the case, and why? Explain that I really, really, *really* did not want to be *NEXT*.

But what about Liz?

I closed my eyes and steadied my breathing. Regardless of whether or not I decided to continue investigating scams, killers and ring-ins— my baby sister was still missing.

The five minute timer dinged, making me jump. I switched the ultrasonic machine off, toweled Lofty's leg dry and settled him back in his kennel with a piece of dried liver. Then I clicked on reply.

Be there in 30 minutes.

While the kettle boiled to make up a thermos of coffee, I showered and changed into clean jeans and sweater and stashed an apple and banana and three large bags of Salt and Vinegar potato chips into my Simpson's backpack. Nothing like potato chips to stave off hunger pangs when on surveillance—and the two pieces of fruit would counteract the calories in the potato chips. Funnily enough, I'd discovered this little pearl of wisdom inside a greasy Teen magazine while waiting at the local fish and chip shop for my five dollars' worth of hot chips.

Turning onto the road leading to Gina's property, I cringed. For some blonde-moment reason, Tanya had parked her car right outside the front gate. The flaming red Yaris couldn't be more conspicuous if it was a wart on the end of a nose. No wonder there'd been no sightings— no bad guys loitering around the house—no sign of Gina doing anything illegal. It was a wonder the feisty GAP coordinator hadn't stormed out to the car and demanded to know what the hell Tanya was up to. Which is probably what Tanya had in mind—when her hormones are in disarray, she loves nothing more than a reason to rumble.

I eased my station wagon onto an empty lot across the road from the surveillance point and parked behind a thick impenetrable bush of some sort—never been good at botanical sounding names—and although I could see Gina's house through a space in the foliage, I was pretty sure she couldn't see me.

"Hey, Tanya," I said calling her on my mobile once I'd switched off the car's ignition. "Anything happened since your last report?"

"Nah. Reckon the wicked witch from Sleeping Beauty cast a spell over the place. I've been twaiting for Prince Charming to ride up on a white horse so I can distract him, by jumping his bones."

Ignoring Tanya's banter, I quickly filled her in on my early morning, spray-can toting, scary-as-hell visitor. Then, how DI Adams had warned me off the case.

"Well, what are you doing here?" Her voice rose four decibels and I held the phone from my ear to stave off deafness. "Just drop it, Kat!" she yelled. "Turn the car around and drive away. We can meet up at the pub and have lunch before I go to work. This is crazy. And…it's—not—your—fight."

"But what about Liz?"

"What about her?"

"Scott's clue points to Liz being at Gina's place."

"Scott? How can you trust the word of a guy who's been in prison?"

"It's all I've got."

She sighed and her voice grew softer. "Let the police handle this, Kat. You don't know for sure that Liz is at Gina's."

"And I don't know that she's not."

There was a short silence on the other end of the phone and I could imagine Tanya wrestling with the problem, hormones inciting her to smash the collective noses of my night-visitor, Liz, Gina and even DI Adams. Then I heard her draw in a quick breath. "Okay," she growled, "but if there's any sign of trouble, ring me, and I'll come back. Do *not* go in there alone."

I smiled. That was the third person today who'd told me to ring if I was in trouble. First, DI Adams, then my gorgeous Ben, who also held me in a hug that warmed my bones and settled the scary chills in my stomach, and now Tanya. With friends like these in my corner—the bad guys didn't stand a chance.

Expecting Tanya to beep her horn at me as she drove past, I watched her start up her car and drive off. No horn and she didn't even glance in my direction. Aha, one day my best friend might make an excellent sleuth's assistant.

I leaned my head back against the head rest and let out a ragged breath. Hey, if I was going to sit here for the next four hours, I may as well relax. Wriggling my bottom into a more comfortable position and stretching out my legs, I reached for the first packet of potato chips.

And that's when Gina burst through her front doorway like a greyhound out of the boxes and sprinted down her driveway.

Oh no! Surely my cover hadn't been blown already. What if she came hurtling across the road, breathing fire, ready to chew me out? Or worse? I hunched down in my seat and held my breath as Gina skidded to a halt on the roadway and stood watching Tanya's Yaris until it turned the corner and disappeared from sight.

Even from my position behind the bushes I could see how jumpy Gina looked. It was written in every line of her body. Normally prepared for a Women's Weekly photo shoot, Gina's hair stood on end, her hands flapped, and her clothes, creased and soiled, looked like she'd slept in them. The moment Tanya's car disappeared, Gina bolted back down the driveway toward the GAP mini-bus parked near her front door. She used the converted mini-bus to pick up greyhounds or transport them to foster homes or take them to shows where their beautiful temperaments could be displayed to prospective new owners.

It was hard to assimilate that Gina, the woman who adored animals, the woman I'd always respected, with a woman who had anything to do with murder and corruption. Was it the thought of big money that tempted her? Pressure from her scruffy new boyfriend?

And where was she off to now?

Key in the ignition, ready to give chase, I watched Gina start up the mini-bus. But instead of heading down the driveway, she rattled and bumped across a neglected paddock covered in stones and high grass and parked the bus in front of a tumbledown shed at the rear of her property. Tucked away behind decades old gum trees and overgrown prickle bushes, the shed, rusty and in need of bulldozing, looked as though it was now only home to spiders, lizards and dirt. So why was Gina parked there? And who or what was inside the shed?

Determined to find out what she was up to, I slipped from the car, scuttled across the road and dived under the fence. Then, using trees and bushes and anything that afforded some form of cover, I crept toward the GAP mini-bus. The thing that struck me as strange was the lack of animals roaming the yard. They must all be locked up. Usually there'd be at least three old dogs wandering around, bantams, a couple of pigs and of course, Atticus the goat. It was almost eerie without them.

With a furtive glance both ways, Gina dragged open the shed door and disappeared inside.

Coast clear, I jogged toward a hundred-year-old ghost gum that shaded the shed and pressed myself behind the tree's enormous girth.

I didn't have long to wait. Within two minutes, Gina, paler than the cartoon Casper, hurried from the shed to the mini-bus, dragging two greyhounds on leads behind her. The dogs looked unsteady on their feet, as though they'd been drugged. I frowned. What was going on? After helping the dogs through the door of the bus, she scooted back into the shed and appeared minutes later with another two dogs.

Bile rose in my throat. Now I understood. The two dogs dragging behind her this time were friends of mine. Stanley and Rambo. Stanley, normally rambunctious and bouncy, could barely put one paw in front of the other and Rambo, the slow snail, lay down and refused to move. Gina had to place an arm under his chest to lift him up and help him to the bus.

Anger, a slow bubbling cauldron, stirred inside me, threatening to turn me into a one-woman police force. Not only was Gina a murderer—she was a fake. She proclaimed herself to be an animal lover, yet she'd used these poor dogs in a racing scam, hidden them on her property, drugged them—and now what? Had she decided to drive them somewhere isolated and dispose of them? I sucked in a huge breath ready to step out from behind the tree and perform a citizen's arrest, preferably by knocking Gina out with one punch, when a second woman appeared from inside the shed with another two dogs in tow, plus Atticus, the goat.

My breath caught in my throat, almost choking me. The second woman—dressed in a long colorful skirt, hem dragging in the dirt, scarf covering her head and neck weighed down with wooden beads of all shapes and colors—was my missing sister, Liz.

"Hey, Gina. Are you sure we need this goat?" she said. "He's a pain in the butt."

"Yes, bring him along. He's a good influence on the dogs. They like the goat and when we get there, he'll keep them calm."

Liz wasn't acting like a kidnap victim. She was as determined as Gina to get the drugged greyhounds into the GAP mini-bus. So if she was here of her own free will—a mere ten minute drive from my house— why hadn't she contacted me?

Unless…

Bile rose in my throat and I leaned my forehead against the smooth bark of the ancient ghost gum.

Oh please, don't let my wacky sister be involved in the *ring-in* scam? Raising money illegally for one of her many environmental causes?

No sooner had that thought burglarized my brain, than another— even more shocking—caused my legs to buckle.

Had Liz been there, in his house, when Jack Lantana was murdered?

26

A TIGHT BAND PRESSED AGAINST MY TEMPLES and I clung to the tree for support. No way would Liz be involved in murder. Geez, stepping on an ant sent her into shrieks of remorse. I'd got it all wrong.

And then my fingers strayed to the bracelet circling my wrist—the bracelet I'd found on Lantana's desk the night Tanya and I were chased into his house by the two guard dogs.

My sister Liz's ruby bracelet.

Had Lantana become violent, threatened her and she retaliated? Had she fought him off, belted him over the head with a dirty great vase and accidentally killed him—then panicked, rung Gina, and for some obscure reason they'd shoved the body in the refrigerator? Or was it the other way around—had Gina caused the blow and Liz come to her rescue?

Almost hyperventilating, I watched the two women settle the animals in the mini-bus and prepare to leave.

"Better grab your backpack, Liz?" said Gina, with another furtive glance over her shoulder. "No way can you come back here after we've dealt with the dogs. It'll be too dangerous."

That was enough for me. It was now or never. Sister or not—I had to come out of hiding and protect the hapless dogs from suffering any more pain.

Both fists tensed ready for conflict, I swept all soft thoughts of my kid sister to the back of my mind where they collided with fantasies of me as a superstar X Factor singer and the one of Hugh Jackman inviting me home for dinner.

Edging around the tree, I could see Gina, head under the hood of the bus, while Liz, back pack swinging, closed the shed door and ran across the grass toward her co-conspirator.

It was time to confront them and find out the truth.

But before I could go into my Xenia Warrior Princess action mode, a quick flash of silver on the far side of the mini-bus distracted me. I paused. Narrowed my eyes and squinted across at the thick tangle of bushes.

There it was again.

Stumbling, I quickly ducked under cover of the tree again as a big dark hulk of a man dressed in a long black coat, stepped from his hiding place and moved silently toward the unsuspecting Liz and Gina. I opened my mouth to call out, warn them—but no sound came out. My voice had decided to go on holiday.

"Going somewhere, ladies?" the man crooned. His voice was soft, flat, and vaguely familiar. The women spun around, fear transforming their faces into chalky masks. When they didn't answer, the man, clearly intent on menace, deliberately flexed both shoulders, cracked his neck and rolled his head from side to side.

I leant against the solid trunk of the tree and closed my eyes. Intent on his two victims, he hadn't seen me—but when he'd turned his head—I'd recognized him.

Receding hairline, wet thick lips, mouth smiling but eyes telling a completely different story…

No wonder his voice sounded familiar. It was Big Mick, the bookie. The same Big Mick I'd had dealings with before. The sleazy bookie who was always on the take.

And the silver flash?

A gun.

Which was now pointing at Gina and Liz.

"Ah. So this is where you've been hiding the evidence?" he said, gesturing toward the shed with the gun. "Even drugged the mongrels so they wouldn't bark and attract attention. Clever." He sniggered, his lips set in a perpetual snarl. "But not clever enough. I've had my eye on you two and knew you'd eventually lead me to the four legged witnesses." He shook his head in mock sympathy. "Can't help yourself, can you Gina? Gotta save every bloody animal on the planet. Even talked Garry Smart, that half-witted boyfriend of yours, into letting you hide the dogs instead of shooting them, like I'd told him to."

Gina dropped the bonnet of the bus into place with a bang and turned to face the man with the gun, her GAP face in place. "Come on, Mick. There's no need to shoot the dogs. Let me place them into the Greyhound Adoption Program. What harm can they do? Dogs can't talk. They can't tell anyone about your racing scam."

He laughed and it wasn't a fun sound. "And what happens when the dye wears off or someone decides to check the mongrels' ear brands, hey?"

"Nothing. The dogs will be with pet owners by then. And what do the general public really know about racing?"

"You seem to be missing the point here, my lovely Gina. I've got too much at stake to pander to you and your hippy friend's pie-in-the-sky, Save the World philosophies. *My* only philosophy is—the world starts with me and mine and that's where it stops."

Liz, mouth set in a straight line, took a step toward him. "If you shoot those dogs, you piece of pig's shit, I'll be the first to talk."

I held my breath. Oh no. Stupid-stupid-stupid. If only I could dash out tuck my sister under my arm and run away—like I did the time she stood up to a bully with a baseball bat when she was five.

Yet I was never more proud of her.

"Is that so?" Mick said and you could have sharpened nails on the tone of his voice. He made a great show of leveling his gun at an invisible X right between Liz's eyes. I opened my mouth to scream as he tightened his trigger finger but he just said BANG and then let out a laugh that would scare the collar off a shirt. "You'll keep. Now, enough chitchat, ladies. Time to move. Okay, Gina, ya'd better tie this mouthy one up and toss her in the back of the bus with the dogs—or I'll put a bullet through her right here and now. And then grab two shovels from the shed and climb in behind the wheel. You're gonna to drive me to an isolated spot I know, where we can...*talk* some more."

I clutched at my chest in an attempt to ease my heart rate down from a million mile an hour to something I could actually live with—and watched Gina, her shoulders slumped in defeat, carry out Big Mick Harrison's orders

*****

I'd lost them.

Crouched over the steering wheel, I strained my eyes to check the vehicles on the bitumen road ahead. I chewed on my bottom lip until I tasted blood.

Where was the GAP mini-bus?

By the time I'd waited until the bus trundled out of Gina's gateway, then raced back to my car to follow—they were nowhere in sight.

Sweat trickled down into my eyes and I dashed it away with the back of my hand. Sweat—or tears?

If I didn't find them…

No, I couldn't think like that. Instead, I pressed my foot down harder on the accelerator and squinted at the vehicles ahead. Surely after Liz and Gina finished digging a hole to bury the dogs Mick would let them go? Or would he? An icicle of fear jammed my arteries and sent my heart racing. No way could Big Mick afford to leave any live witnesses. With seven kids all under the age of eight—Big Mick Harrison would do whatever it took to keep himself out of prison.

One hand on the wheel, I fumbled my mobile phone open, discovered there was only one bar left on my battery, tossed six identical F words out into the Universe, and sent a text message to Tanya.

Big Mick the killer. Taken Liz and Gina. I'm following.

I switched off the phone, clutched the wheel more tightly and drove to Port Wakefield road where I turned right. Figured Mick would be heading away from the city—he'd mentioned an isolated spot he knew—so he'd be more likely traveling on the highway to the north.

And there it was—about a mile ahead of me—with its white body, red printing and colorful paintings of greyhounds adorning the sides and rear—the GAP mini-bus. And it was bowling along, right on the speed limit. Of course Mick wouldn't want to attract any police presence by speeding. But hey—not me. I'd welcome the police with a great big hug. Aiming to catch up, I jammed my foot on the accelerator and zoomed through traffic, deflecting and ignoring car horns and irate drivers' middle fingers, until I was only three cars behind.

Content to stay where I could keep an eye on the bus without drawing attention to myself, I slowed down, snatched my phone from on top of the console and switched it on again.

Damn. One bar and wavering.

I sent another frantic text to Tanya: *Heading north on Port Wakefield road,* and switched the phone off again.

Half hour later, the Gap mini-bus turned off the main road onto a dirt track, heading toward the beach. I slowed down and followed, making sure I kept well to the rear. Hopefully Mick would be too busy concentrating on his present plan to look in the rear vision mirror. Even if he did, I doubt he'd recognize my car. Probably think it was some guy heading off for a spot of fishing.

I turned my phone on again and a text message beeped up straight away. Yay! It was from Ben. Then another identical message came through from DI Adams.

Where r u now?

I let out a whoop. The rescue team of DI Adams, Ben and Tanya were on their way. Big Mick Harrison wouldn't stand a chance against my team.

First dirt road on left after Port Wakefield.

I clicked on 'send' and the screen on my phone went blank.

Nooooo!

Willing the message to get through, I banged the phone against the consul. I sent screaming vibes into the Universe. I cursed. I yelled.

Not now. Please…please…not now.

How could my rescue team save Liz and Gina if they didn't know where to look?

Of course the answer to that question left me shaking so much I skidded across the road and had to haul hard on the wheel to straighten the car out again.

The answer was—they couldn't…

So now, it was all up to me.

27

My car juddered down the dirt road, the ancient shockers complaining at every bounce. In a daze, I gripped the steering wheel harder. If only this was a bad dream. A bad dream where I'd wake up hot and sweaty and tangled in my bed sheets—but knowing I would feel better after two cups of coffee and a plate of scrambled eggs.

All up to me...

The words crashed around in my head as I drove, threatening to fuse my brain cells and create an electrical short. I shook myself. Snatched a quick breath.

You are all that stands between the murderer and your sister—so for goodness sake stop acting like a floppy rag doll and get your act together.

Okay, I needed a plan. Not just any old plan but a plan huge enough to outwit the man with the gun and rescue his two-legged and four-legged victims.

I closed my eyes. Hell, I didn't need a plan—I needed a gold plated miracle. Firstly, Mick was bigger than me by about eight inches and ten stone. And secondly, Mick had a gun. And what did I bundle into my back pack whilst preparing for surveillance? Coffee and potato chips. I sighed and tried to imagine a scene that included death by potato chips. A scene where I threw hot coffee in Mick's face and while he was recovering, shoved handfuls of potato chips down his throat until he choked to death.

Resisting the urge to bang my forehead against the steering wheel, I let out another colorful curse, opened my eyes and quickly brought the car back under control. If I didn't concentrate on my driving I'd be a mangled wreck on the side of the road and of no use to anyone.

Plus…while my eyes had been closed, the GAP mini-bus had disappeared. There was no sign of it on the road up ahead.

Figuring Mick had directed Gina to drive the bus off the road, I slowed down so I could peer into the scrub, searching amongst the prickle bushes and undulating sand hills. The wind whipped loose sand in the air and it pelted the roof and sides of the car as though warning me to go home—I was no match for Big Mick and his deadly gun.

Five hundred yards further down the road I came to a grinding halt. Was that the white nose of the GAP mini-bus protruding from behind a dense thicket of scrub?

One eye on the mini-bus, I cautiously eased the car off the road and ploughed through the heavy sand until I came to a well-concealed dip a couple of hundred meters further on. Heart pounding, I switched off the ignition and sat and waited. Two minutes passed. When no bullets whizzed past the windscreen, no big hulking man in a black coat jumped out of the bushes, I decided to open the car door and climb out.

Now what?

Eyes and ears on high alert, I edged my way toward the bus. No humans in sight, only the six dogs with their noses plastered against the windows. Okay, the dogs' eyes still appeared a little foggy but they seemed more on the ball than when they left Gina's property. And most importantly—they were still alive.

One hand on the bus door ready to open it, I was distracted by Gina's voice coming from the other side of the sand hill.

"Come on, Mick. You're not a bad man. You don't really want to do this."

I threw myself down on my stomach and quickly wriggled to the top of the hill where I eased my head over the top and took in the scene below. If I was lucky enough to live through this nightmare, the scene below would keep me awake at night for years to come.

Gina, breathing heavily, was looking pleadingly up at Mick while Liz, hair plastered to her face, leant on her shovel and examined the toes of her boots. They both stood knee high in a newly dug hole. My stomach cramped. How much deeper did the hole have to be? Deep enough to bury six dogs? Or deep enough for six dogs and two humans?

Big Mick, his face impassive, long black coat making him look like the harbinger of Death stood, legs apart, gun steady, a few feet away. Where was the loving father who played ball, helped feed the triplets, kissed his kids goodnight? I didn't know this man.

And I was fast running out of time.

Mick waved his gun in the air. "You're wrong there, Gina. I *do* want to do this. Now shut up and save your breath for digging. Fair dinkum, you're using that shovel like a bloody tooth pick. Put your back into it or I'll shoot your mouthy friend and you'll have to finish digging the hole on your own."

"Well," put in her mouthy friend, aka my brainless sister, "if you don't like the way we're digging, why don't you dig the bloody hole yourself?"

A reluctant grin spread across Mick's face. "You've got a bit of an attitude there, kiddo, but unfortunately for you, it's slowing you down. Now, the way I see it, you have two choices—either put your back into it and dig the hole willingly, or I'll put a bullet in your foot and you'll be digging up your own blood."

"Come on, Liz," said Gina wiping sweat from her forehead with the sleeve of her sweater. "Don't antagonize the bastard. You'll only make this more fun for him."

The two bent to their task again and Mick regained his stance of legs apart, gun at the ready.

My stomach roiled. I knew as soon as the hole was deep enough Mick would shoot the dogs and order Gina and Liz to bury them.

And then what?

Okay, one thing at a time—first, I'd rescue the dogs.

I slid down the sand hill and approached the bus, praying the dogs wouldn't bark and give me away. All okay. With the drug still in their system they didn't seem to have the energy to do more than slobber on the window when they saw me coming.

Stanley was the first to greet me when I opened the door of the mini-bus. Staggering up from the back of the bus like a drunk, he cleaned my face with his tongue and then promptly fell over.

"Hi sweetie. Good to see you too," I whispered, helping him to his feet and deciding to transfer the dogs to my car. If I let them loose in the scrub they might wander onto the road and become road-kill. Or cause an accident if a driver swerved to miss them. If I stashed them in my car, at least that would slow Big Mick down.

As I helped the dogs out of the bus, Attica the goat pushed past and launched himself at me.

"Hey!" I hissed trying to get out of his way. "Watch it buddy!"

Disregarding my whispered warning he butted me in the chest, grinned in satisfaction and then took off into the scrub.

Now *that* one I wasn't worried about. Bloody Attica could look after himself.

Whatever drug Gina fed the six greyhounds to keep them quiet had also affected their coordination. But at last, after much manhandling, I managed to steer each dog across the sand to my car. Squeezing six fully grown greyhounds into a station wagon was a bit like packing sardines in a tin, but once inside, the dogs seemed happy enough to scrunch up and go back to sleep. At least five of them did. Stanley, after licking my face, turned in a tight circle then proceeded to sprawl out comfortably across the entire front seat of my car.

How could Mick even contemplate shooting these gorgeous animals?

Dogs settled, I scuttled back to the bus, intent on finding a weapon to defend myself against the enemy. Seemed like Gina wasn't afraid of hold-ups or muggings as there was no knife—no gun—not even a sharp nail file to be found. All I could rustle up was a rusty tire iron. So with the rough steel pressed hard against the palm of my hand, I set off to climb the sand hill again.

Flat on my stomach, I peered over the crest of the hill. Oh! Uh! The hole was bigger now. *Much, much, bigger.* The ticking clock was fast approaching zero hour. I wriggled forward. My plan was to inch down the hill and approach Mick from behind, belt him over the head with the tire iron, tie him up while he was unconscious, and then rescue Liz and Gina.

Easy.

A couple of feet down the slope, doubts crept in and my plan started to crumble around the edges. Mick was a lot taller than me. Even if I did manage to get behind him without him noticing, would my arm be long enough to reach high enough and bring the tire iron down hard enough to knock him out?

Oh God. And what if he spotted the loose sand shimmering down the hill every time I moved?

Damn. This wasn't going to work. I stopped, snatched a reassuring breath and went searching for my inner strength, screaming in my head at the Universe to get his/her butt out here and give me a helping hand.

"You'll never get away with this, you piece of dog's shit." That was my sister, taking a rest from digging, but not from aggravating the man with the gun.

"Ah, but I will." The man with the gun twisted his mouth into a semblance of a smile. Reminded me of a fat snake with the gastro virus. "In fact, I reckon that hole is large enough now to start eliminating the evidence."

"Nooo!" yelled Gina. "Don't shoot the dogs, Mick. They won't talk. I'll send them to an interstate GAP program. No-one will ever know."

"Except you and the mouthy one."

His words hung in the air. Implying what?

Oh God, it was time for action. Now or never. I quickly pushed myself into a crouching position and slithered out from behind the covering bushes ready to continue my descent.

Didn't see the rabbit hole.

Didn't mean to lose my balance.

And with a shriek of dismay, went tumbling head over turkey down the hill.

When I finally lifted my nose from the sand and gazed upward, three pair of wide startled eyes greeted me.

But it was the black eyes of the killer that made me want to vomit.

28

I spat the sand from my mouth, gingerly touched my right eye which felt like it had come in contact with a rock the size of Uluru, and sat up. My head ached. And when I moved my legs, a searing pain shot through my right ankle. Great. Just when I might be called on to run for my life—I'd sprained my freakin' ankle.

"Nice of you to drop in, Katrina." Mick's voice, colder than steel, conveyed exactly how welcome I was at his little hole-digging ceremony.

"Where in heavens did you spring from?" Gina bent to help me to my feet but one Rottweiler snarl from the man with the gun had her backing off in a hurry.

I dragged my eyes away from Mick and Gina and stared at Liz. My little sister. Face smeared with sweat and dirt, the hem of her long colorful skirt torn, hands bleeding from digging, she stared back at me as though I was a gourmet ice cream and she wanted to eat me in one big swallow.

Finally, she dropped her eyes to her feet and sighed. "Hi, Kat."

"Hi, Kat?" I snapped. Suddenly the hurt of Liz's rejection overflowed, pushing aside the fear of the man with the gun. "That all you can say after six years of avoiding me?"

"Well, what do you *want* me to say?"

"Damn it, Liz. I'm your sister—once your best friend and protector—and yet after Dad died you took off and left me to cope with Ma on my own."

"You know what she was like with me, Kat. With Daddy gone—I couldn't cope. I had to get away."

"Okay, so what about now?" I demanded. "Gina lives a few blocks from me and yet you couldn't pick up the phone—or say—drop around to *see* me—let me know you weren't lying dead in a gutter somewhere."

She shrugged one shoulder and her face closed down. "I didn't contact you, Kat, because I knew this was how you'd carry on."

I let out a gasp of disbelief. "I *carry on* as you call it, because—"

"*Enough!*" yelled Mick, spittle flying from his mouth. "Jesus, it was trouble enough having the Mouthy One in my ear every five minutes—now I have her freakin' sister too. Kat McKinley, what the hell are you doing here?"

"I followed you."

"Oh, did you now? Can't say I'm surprised though," he said, eyes shooting daggers at me—every one razor sharp and itching to slice me into tiny bite-sized pieces. "You're always poking your nose in where it's not wanted. Reckon you're some bloody great sleuth, don't you? A girly Sherlock Holmes?" He lifted his lip in a sneer as I tried to push to my knees and let out a yelp of pain. "Well, you're not. You're nothing but a freakin' snoop."

"I—"

"But this time, Katrina," he broke in, his voice like chalk on a blackboard, "you stuck your nose into *my* business." Two black holes of death stared chillingly back at me as Mick's gun shifted closer, his finger quivering on the trigger. "And *that* means I can't let you walk away from here."

I stared at the gun, mesmerized. I was going to die, yet my throat was suddenly too dry, too closed over with fear to do what all fictional heroines always do in mystery novels—keep the bad guy talking. Hell, my throat was too dry to even gulp.

But not so, Gina's. "For God's sake, Mick, stop this nonsense and come to your senses before it's too late. Think of your family."

Mick gave a mirthless laugh. "This *is* about my family, Gina. The bookmaking business isn't what it used to be and I've had a long run of losses. How do you feed a wife and seven kids when there's no money coming in? Beg on the streets?"

"But you don't want to add *murder* to your list of crimes."

His laugh was off-key, almost over the edge. "Who do you think did away with Jack Lantana, that idiot with the fashion sense of a 60s rock groupie?" Mick gave another hysterical laugh—but at least his gun shifted away from me which meant I could start breathing again. "Did you know, Lantana demanded a bigger cut of the profits? As if. Hell, I did the world a favor when I took him out. The decrepit old guy had the brain capacity of a lump of wood."

"And what about Scott?" Liz edged forward. "You tried to kill him too, didn't you?"

"His own fault. Scott overheard me talking to my mate, Garry Smart, so he had to go. In between races, Garry slipped a little something into Scott's drink and then offered to help him to his car when he started feeling dizzy." Mick turned his head in my direction and snarled. "It was a fool-proof plan too. Would have worked—except Sleuth Girl here stuck her nose in—*again*."

I sent him the sweetest smile I could dredge up under the circumstances. "That's okay, Mick. Anyone in a similar situation would have done the same thing."

The snarl changed to a roar.

"So, Garry was involved in attempted murder?" Gina's voice grated against her throat, each word forced through gritted teeth.

Mick tutted. "Gina, your boyfriend has been in this up to his foul-smelling armpits since the beginning."

"The pathetic little creep." Gina let out a sigh. "And he isn't my boyfriend—he's my stepbrother. Ever since he came into my life at fifteen, he's been trouble. Got let out of jail a couple of months ago and came whining to me for help."

"And helping him was your first mistake," said Mick. "The whole scam was Garry's idea in the first place. He owed me fifty thousand dollars in gambling debts and couldn't pay, so the Slow Dog scam was a way out for him."

"I'm just as pathetic for believing him. He swore on his mother's grave that he was trying to go straight. Said some guy had forced him to steal greyhounds and would kill him if he refused. I told him I'd dob him in unless he brought the dogs to me so I could hide them and eventually get them into GAP homes."

"And that decision landed you right smack in the middle of the scam."

While Gina continued to distract Mick, I transferred my weight to my hands and pushed upwards, attempting to stand. Wrong move. Immediately the nose of the gun swung around and pressed against my left temple. I froze, still kneeling in the sand, the pain in my ankle making me want to cry.

In my peripheral vision I could see Liz, shovel half-raised, inching forward.

But so could Mick.

His eyes never leaving my face, he dug the gun harder into my head. "If your mouthy sister takes one more step, we'll see daylight through the hole in your head, Katrina. And of course there'll be a matching hole in hers too. Which of course will only leave Gina and me to get rid of the dogs. Still, no big deal. I'm tired of playing games and don't need all this irritation."

Gina threw her shovel in the hole and stood, head up, shoulders back. "Shoot my friends, Mick, and you may as well shoot me too because I'm not going to lift a finger to help you harm the dogs."

The gun moved slowly in Gina's direction. "In that case, I'll shoot you first."

A whirlwind of white fur broke through the clump of bushes directly behind Mick. A four-legged flash of white, armed with a smug grin and with only one objective in mind.

"Hey, how do you like your goat steaks, Mick?" I said, grinning inanely up at him as he stood, black coat wrapped around him, completely unaware of his fate.

"What—"

I held my breath as Atticus the goat, horns lowered, grin fixed in place, aimed for the most vulnerable spot at the back of Mick's knees.

Bull's eye.

The gun flew in the air. I reached out with one hand and grabbed it on its way down, and Liz swung her shovel in the direction of our captor's head and connected as he catapulted past.

"Yay!" I yelled, waving the gun.

"Woohoo!" said Liz, waving her shovel.

"Good boy," said Gina, cuddling the goat whose rough tongue was busy cleaning the dirt from her face.

I painfully climbed to my feet, leant against Liz for support and we all stood and silently regarded the fallen bookie as he lay at the bottom of the hole.

If Atticus hadn't come to our rescue, this man—a cold blooded killer—would have shot the dogs, forced us to bury them and then shot us too.

I shivered.

You couldn't always tell what evil stirred in another person's mind.

Okay, I'd never regarded Big Mick as a friend, and he'd always put his hand up to participate in any money-making scam, but—a killer? No way. An image of Mick's children eating at the kitchen table sprang to mind. Five still in high chairs—a giggling baby Eddy throwing spaghetti. How would these children feel in years to come when the kids at school teased them, called their father a murderer?

He deserved everything the court threw at him.

I raised the gun. Cocked it. "Okay, scumbag," I said as I pointed the gun at a vulnerable spot between Big Mick's legs. "Just move ya little pinkie finger—and your family jewels are history."

I could hear several police sirens wailing in the distance and looked up as a four wheel drive pulled off the road and came bumping across the sand toward us. It screeched to a halt and out tumbled Detective Sergeant Adams followed by Ben and Tanya.

I grinned like an insane Cheshire Cat at the sight of the three people I most wanted to see. "So, you *did* get my message."

"Yep, but it seems like you and the girls have everything under control," said Ben. "We're just in time to applaud." He smiled at me, a smile so warm and tender, I had to swallow to stop myself from crying. Still smiling, he hurried over and slipped an arm around my waist, pulling me tight against his body to plant a kiss on my nose. "You okay, babe?"

"Sprained ankle, that's all."

Tanya, eyes bulging, stared, horrified, at the body lying at the bottom of the hole. When she spoke, her voice was barely above a whisper. "Is he dead?"

We stood in a circle around the hole, all eying Mick. Twenty seconds passed and no-one spoke.

At last, I shook my head. "Well, *I'm* not volunteering to go down there to find out."

"Of course not, Ms. McKinley," said Detective Adams, harrumphing and evidently deciding it was time he took charge of the situation. "This is police business now."

"What I mean is, I couldn't anyway—can't walk—hurt my ankle when I went for a tumble down the hill," I said waving the gun in the air to demonstrate how I rolled over and over when I lost my footing.

Adams turned white, gasped, and then ducked. "For God's sake, give me that gun before it goes off."

"Here, take it." I shoved the gun in his direction, then winced as the detective ducked again. "Sorry."

Adams snatched the gun and disposed of the bullets. "Fine," he said. "Now, stand back and leave this to me." While reading the comatose man his rights and fumbling in his many pockets for his set of handcuffs, Adams slid down into the hole. We watched as he bent forward, attached handcuffs to the man's wrists and then felt for a pulse. Finally, he looked up and nodded. "He's alive," he said. "But whoever hit him must have given him a decent old whack. This man's out for the count."

Gina and I turned to Liz and gave her a high five. She laughed and the tension drizzled out of me.

"Yep! My sister, by a knockout!"

29

It was a week since Big Mick Harrison had been arrested and thrown in jail. I stood at the front door of my house, a crutch digging into my armpit, my back resting against Ben's six-pack stomach and saying goodbye to the family who'd adopted Stanley.

The endearing GAP greyhound trotted down the path toward the unfamiliar bright yellow family station wagon. Every now and again he'd cock his head to one side as though listening intently to something the ten-year-old boy on the other end of the lead said to him. Earlier the pair had been rough housing on my back lawn, yet the moment the boy's eighteen month old sister toddled out to play, Stanley froze, then sauntered across, licked her face and when she plopped down on her rear end, lay beside her, head in her lap. That was the cincher. The Murphy family couldn't get the dog's collar and lead on quickly enough. They signed the GAP papers and paid the fee and now the exuberant greyhound with the heart of a marshmallow was off to his new home with his brand new adoptive family.

"Alone, at last," Ben growled in my ear. A growl that caused goose bumps to spring up along my bare arms and other unmentionable places. "Now, how long did you say that sister of yours would be gone? Was it in two or three hours?" Ben bent to nibble on one of my earlobes while I forced my hand to continue waving at the yellow car now pulling out of the gateway.

When his soft nibbles became tiny fairy flicks of the tongue, my legs turned into lettuce leaves. And if I hadn't leaned heavily against Ben's chest, I'd have melted into a puddle at his feet.

"Liz and Jake are at the local hospital protesting about the new parking meters," I murmured, repositioning my head to one side for easier ear access. "Could be gone for the rest of the day."

"Hmm. That long, hey?" Ben slowly spun me around to face him, rescued my tumbling crutch at the last minute and propped it up against the door. "So…with all that time to kill—how about we do an in-depth study of positions one to twenty of the *Kama Sutra*?"

"Only one to twenty?" I grinned. "My Grandma McKinley always insists it's practice that makes perfect."

"Your grandma is a very wise woman, Katrina," Ben purred as he bent forward to tease my lips with his oh-so-tantalizing tongue. A tongue that would have won any reality show's Sexiest Tongue contest. Instead it was mine.

All mine.

Clinging to Ben for support, I groaned my surrender, softened my lips and sucked the heat of all that desire into my mouth. Ben aligned his body against mine, his tongue exploring every intimate crevice inside my mouth, his hands under my T-shirt, inside my bra, cupping my breast, thumb circling the engorged nipples.

There was a damp spot spreading between my legs. A damp spot that needed urgent, immediate attention.

Gasping, I pulled away, fitted the crutch under my armpit and slammed the front door. "Hang on, I'll just give Tater and Lucky a handful of kibble each and shut them outside."

"Gotcha." There was a spot of drool in one corner of Ben's lips and I swear the pupils in both eyes were dilated. "I'll dig out a bottle of Chardonnay and fluff up the cushions on the sofa."

I almost tripped in my hurry to reach the kitchen. Hell, this was the first time in the last week Ben and I had been alone. No way was I going to waste one precious minute. Between Liz staying with me until my ankle healed, DI Adams swooping in and out asking questions, Tanya popping in to fill me in on her love life—yeah, she and Paul Simmons, the cop, had actually been together for three whole weeks now—and Gina helping with my greyhounds while I recovered from my ankle sprain, there hadn't been an opportunity for more than a few stolen kisses.

"Did you know they've caught up with Gina's stepbrother, Garry?" I yelled from the kitchen. "He was hitch-hiking his way up North and got picked up by an off duty cop. Not what you'd call the luckiest guy on the planet."

"Has Liz heard from Scott?"

"Yeah," I said collecting the two dog dishes and a box of kibble from the cupboard. "He's in the clear with the police. Should be out of hospital in a few days."

"And—"

"He's going home to recuperate at his parent's house until he's stronger. Seems the carbon monoxide affected his lungs."

"Another charge against Big Mick and Garry."

Dodging Tater, who was ordering me to hurry up with the grub, I called Lucky and let both dogs outside.

"Be good now," I told them both, then poured kibble into their bowls and left them to their morning snack.

The moment I hopped back inside, Ben grabbed me. "Come here, wench," he growled, kissing me firmly on the mouth, then, holding me by the shoulders he regarded me, his expression serious. "Kat, have you ever done it in the lotus position?"

"The *what*?" I laughed and shook my head. "Ben, I am *not* attempting anything resembling a lotus position on that narrow couch. One sprained ankle for the week is enough, thank you very much."

Before I could take a breath, he'd nudged my wooden crutch away with his foot, scooped me into his arms and started for the stairs. "In that case, my gammy-legged wench, let's proceed to the queen sized bed."

A scattering of gravel outside indicated a car had pulled up out the front. Ben let out a groan and closed his eyes. I could hear Liz laughing and the sound of Jake talking as they approached the front door.

"How long did you say your sister was staying?" Ben asked through gritted teeth.

"As long as she wants," I confessed.

I heard the front door crash against the wall as it was flung open. "Hey, Kat," Liz called out. "Where are you? We're back! Protest was called off. Stupid council backed down before Jake and I could even chain ourselves to the parking meters."

Defeated, I let my head drop onto my chest.

"You know," whispered Ben, a grin tugging at the corner of his lips as, still carrying me, he turned and tiptoed toward the back door. "My car is parked around the back"

"It is?"

"Yep. And what's more, I have a top of the range queen sized bed in my caravan, at home."

"You do?" I whispered, my arms tightening around his neck as I leant down, turned the knob to open the back door so the dogs could come in and we could sneak out.

"There's even fresh sheets on the bed and a deadlock on the caravan door."

"Mmm. Sounds perfect."

"No, what I call perfect is the fact that I have a *second* copy of the *Kama Sutra* stashed in my sock drawer. Right next to the condoms."

I let out a contented sigh and snuggled closer.

Now what could be more *puuurfect* than that?

Dear Readers

A former school teacher, competitive horse rider, and greyhound trainer, June Whyte has always dreamed of being an author.

She wrote her first full-length story (with chapters) when she was nine-years-old — *Donald McDonald in Texas* — a story involving a rather extraordinary boy who rode buck-jumpers in a rodeo.

And when she penned her first murder mystery, *Murder Behind Bars*, it resulted in her fifth-grade teacher questioning her home life.

Even now, in retirement, June's favorite spot is sitting in front of her computer, drawing on her knowledge of greyhounds and horses to create humorous mysteries for both adults and younger teens.

Her *Kat McKinley* greyhound series, starting with *Chasing Can Be Murder*, is laugh out loud funny, as is her *Chiana Ryan*, PI, Young Adult mystery series.

She's also written the cozy mystery series, *Vets2U*, which is similar to the TV show, Rosemary & Thyme — but instead of gardeners, Emily and Maggie are veterinarians. This series is for animal lovers — especially those who love horses.

For more information and news, go to:

www.junewhytebooks.com

Thank you,
June Whyte

www.ingramcontent.com/pod-product-compliance
Lightning Source LLC
Chambersburg PA
CBHW032303310726
48973CB00008B/2512